PROFESSOR CHILDERMASS SMILED MYSTERIOUSLY. . . .

"Nobody knows what happened to Father Baart," he said somberly. "One morning he didn't show up to say Mass in the church, and people got worried. His house-keeper and some other people went to the rectory and searched all the rooms, but he was gone. He was never seen again . . . not *alive*, anyway."

Johnny looked puzzled. "You mean they found his body?"

The professor shook his head and smiled tantalizingly. "No. I didn't mean that . . ."

THE CURSE OF THE BLUE FIGURINE

"Spellbinding . . . Bellairs's characters are irresistible and so are the flashes of humor that brighten the macabre doings."—*Publishers Weekly*

"Another of Bellairs's nicely shivery magic tales . . . Bellairs handles the snug suspense expertly, never confounding the reader's expectations, but fulfilling them with communicable relish." —*Kirkus Reviews*

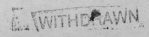

THE CURSE
OF THE
BLUE FIGURINE

JOHN BELLAIRS

A BANTAM SKYLARK BOOK®
TORONTO · NEW YORK · LONDON · SYDNEY · AUCKLAND

This low-priced Bantam Book
contains the complete text of
the original hard-cover edition.
NOT ONE WORD HAS BEEN OMITTED.

RL 6, 009–013

THE CURSE OF THE BLUE FIGURINE
A Bantam Book / published by arrangement with
Dail Books for Young Readers

PRINTING HISTORY
Dail edition published May 1983
Bantam Skylark edition / July 1984
Cover art and frontispiece by Edward Gorey

Skylark Books is a registered trademark of Bantam Books, Inc.
Registered in U.S. Patent and Trademark Office and elsewhere.

ISBN 0-553-15282-3

Published simultaneously in the United States and Canada

Bantam Books are published by Bantam Books, Inc. Its trade-
mark, consisting of the words "Bantam Books" and the por-
trayal of a rooster, is Registered in U.S. Patent and Trademark
Office and in other countries. Marca Registrada. Bantam
Books, Inc., 666 Fifth Avenue, New York, New York 10103.

PRINTED IN THE UNITED STATES OF AMERICA

O   0 9 8 7 6 5 4 3 2 1

For Gerry, who knows about ushabtis

The Curse of
the Blue Figurine

CHAPTER ONE

It was a cold winter evening in January. The year was 1951. A short, pale, bespectacled boy named Johnny Dixon was sitting in a big comfy easy chair in the parlor of his grandparents' house. Outside, it was snowing. Through the bay window you could see the flakes falling. The room was dark except for the faint yellow light that shone from the fan-shaped dial on the front of the big walnut Atwater Kent table-model radio that was next to the easy chair. Johnny's eyes were wide open. He was staring into the darkness and listening intently to the program. On his lap was a plate of Ritz crackers spread with pink pimiento-flavored cream cheese—Johnny always munched while he listened to the radio. This evening he was listening to one of his favorite programs,

The House of Mystery. In this episode Sir Philip Stapleton, the renowned archeologist, had entered the forbidden temple of Kali in the jungles of India. With him was Inspector Marcus Quaterly of Scotland Yard, who had traveled all the way from London to help Professor Stapleton unravel the mystery of the savage killings that had plagued Delhi recently. The temple was dark. Each footstep that the two men took raised endless sinister echoes. Suddenly at the far end of the pillared hall something began to glow eerily. It was a huge golden statue of the four-armed goddess Kali. Now, as the two men stood frozen in their tracks, the statue began to move its arms slowly back and forth. And a hideous croaking voice chanted:

Yaa-maaa
Yaa-maaa

Professor Stapleton's voice was an incredulous gasp. "What is it? What can it mean?"

Inspector Quaterly answered grimly, "*Yama* means death—it means death!" And then . . .

"Johnny! Johnny! Didn't you hear me? I've called you three times! Your grampa 'n' I are waitin', and your dinner's gettin' cold!"

Johnny looked up, startled. He really hadn't heard his grandmother calling. With a sad sigh he turned off the radio. He got up and brushed away some cracker crumbs. Then, meekly, with the plate in his hand, he followed his grandmother out to the dining room.

A few minutes later Johnny was sitting at the big mahogany dining room table with his grandfather and grandmother. As usual Grampa sat at the end by the window, in the chair with the arms. Grampa was a tall, slightly stooped old man who always wore gray work shirts and gray wash pants. He had a high, freckled forehead, and on his big sunburnt nose was perched a pair of gold-rimmed glasses. A few strands of white hair were strung carefully across the top of his head. Loose wrinkled flesh hung down in wattles from his cheeks, and his large hands were covered with brown freckles. Grampa was seventy-four years old. He was old, but he was cheerful—most of the time. He sang songs like "Oh, Susanna!" and "Peter Gray," and went on long walks all over the town with Johnny. He listened to baseball games with Johnny and helped him with his homework and played checkers and cribbage with him. Grampa was a good egg. He was almost like a father to Johnny, which was a good thing because (these days) he was just about the only father that Johnny had. And Gramma—for that matter—was the only mother he did have.

Up until about six months before, Johnny had lived in New York State, in the town of Riverhead on Long Island. But then his mother got sick and died of cancer. At first it seemed to Johnny as if the world had come to an end. Then, as the shock and grief wore off, he began to think that he was getting used to the idea of living alone with his dad. But the Korean War changed things. Johnny's father had been a bomber pilot during World

War II. So the Air Force asked Mr. Dixon to come back and serve again, this time as a jet pilot. Mr. Dixon could have refused. He was the sole surviving parent of a child under the age of eighteen. But Mr. Dixon was itching to get into the cockpit of a fighter plane. And when he found out that Gramma and Grampa Dixon would be glad to take care of Johnny, his mind was made up. So Johnny went north, to the town of Duston Heights, Massachusetts, to live with his grandparents. It had been hard for Johnny to adjust to his new surroundings. He felt lonely a lot of the time, and he was also a little scared. But Gramma and Grampa had been as nice as they could be to him, and that helped a lot.

Johnny smiled happily as Gramma spooned mashed potatoes onto his plate. It was snowing outside, but it was warm and comfy in the big old house. A coal fire was roaring in the furnace in the basement, and the register in the floor breathed warm air into the room. The black Sessions clock on the sideboard ticked quietly and reassuringly. The dining room table was covered with a white linen cloth, and on it were good things to eat: roast beef, cabbage salad, mashed potatoes, and plenty of thick dark-brown gravy. And for dessert there would be either chocolate pudding or lemon meringue pie. The food that Gramma Dixon made tended to be the same, day after day, but it was always good.

As they ate, Gramma and Grampa talked quietly. Sometimes they talked about things that Johnny liked to talk about, but this evening they were chewing over some local gossip, about what so-and-so down the street was doing. Johnny thought all this was very dull, so he just munched and drank and went back to living in his own little dream world. He thought about how great it would be to be an archeologist. That was what he wanted to be, right now, more than anything in the world. He imagined himself with a pith helmet on his head and a pickax in his hand, wading through sand while the hot sun sizzled in the sky. Or exploring by moonlight, which was much more dramatic. Johnny saw himself wandering among the columned halls of the temple of Dendur or Karnak at night, when a pale, silvery sheen fell upon the mysterious hieroglyphs and the carved shapes of pharaohs and beast-headed gods. Was there danger here? Who could tell? What if a shape wrapped in tattered bandages stepped from the shadows and confronted him? What would Professor John Wellesley Dixon, Ph.D., do? Of course there was the large British Army service revolver in the holster that hung from his belt. But it would not be of much use against . . .

The doorbell rang.

Once again Johnny was jolted out of his daydream. He glanced quickly toward the front hall. Gramma heaved a deep, discontented sigh. "Lord, I wonder who *that* is?" She hated to be interrupted during meals.

"I'll go see," said Grampa. He shoved his chair back and got up.

"Me too," said Johnny. He got up and followed his grandfather out to the front door. He really had no reason to go along, but he went anyway, out of sheer uncontrollable curiosity.

Grampa pulled at the front door, and it opened with a rattle. There on the snowy porch stood Professor Childermass. Professor Roderick Childermass, Ph.D., to be precise. Professor Childermass was a short, elderly, red-faced man. A wild nest of white hair covered the top of his head, and mutton-chop whiskers sprouted from the sides of his face. His nose was red and pitted and reminded Johnny of a strawberry. Perched slightly askew on the professor's head was an old shapeless gray fedora, and thrown over his shoulders—sort of like a cape—was an unbelievably dirty and threadbare tweed overcoat. In his left hand the professor clutched a shovel—or what had once been a shovel. It had been one of those little collapsible shovels that the Army calls "an entrenching tool." But the red-colored blade had been battered into a shapeless mass of metal, and the hinged wooden handle was splintered and almost broken in two.

"I am so angry that I can't see straight!" the professor announced through clenched teeth. "I'm so angry that I'd like to *murr-der* someone!"

Grampa couldn't help grinning. He and the professor were old friends. They had had many heated arguments about politics and life and things in general and had always managed to stay friends. Grampa knew that the professor was basically a very kindly man, although he had a rotten temper. Johnny did not know the professor quite as well. He had seen him a few times on the street, and he was—to tell the truth—a bit scared of him. But when he saw his Grampa smiling in such a friendly way, he figured the professor must be an okay person.

"So you wanta murder somebody?" said Grampa, still grinning. "Are you gonna start with the two of us and then work your way down the block? From the way things look," he added, pointing to the shovel, "you've already got started. Who was it? Mrs. Kovacs? Or didja get a cop?"

"Oh, shut up," muttered the professor. He scowled at the broken shovel. "Just you shut up. I destroyed this thing by beating it against the fire hydrant outside my house. I am mad because my car is stuck in the snow and I can't get it out. I've tried everything. I've dug, I've rocked the car, I've . . . oh, drat! Just drat! Can I come in and get warm?"

"Sure," said Grampa, chuckling. "Anything to keep you from standin' there in the doorway and lettin' the cold air in. Come on out to the dinin' room and I'll getcha a cuppa coffee. Then, when you're all thawed out, we'll go get your dad-blasted car outa the dad-blasted snowbank. Okay?"

"Thanks," said the professor stiffly. He stalked through the hall and into the house without taking off his hat, his coat, or his galoshes. As he went he left big gobs of melting snow behind him. *Uh oh,* thought Johnny, *Gramma is gonna have a fit.* Gramma was one of those fussy types who vacuum the house twice a day. She was always dusting and picking up and emptying wastebaskets and ashtrays. Johnny watched with amusement and horror as Professor Childermass stomped to the dining room table and sat down.

"Evening, ma'am," he said, nodding curtly to Gramma. "Just go on with your dinner. Don't mind me." He leaned forward, put his elbows on the table, stared off into space, and began to hum tunelessly. Humming was what he always did when he was trying to cheer himself up after losing his temper.

"Professor Childermass," Gramma said in a biting tone, "do you think you could manage to go out to the front hall and take off your galoshes?"

The professor looked startled, and then he looked sheepish. He glanced hurriedly at his feet and got up. "Excuse me, madam," he said hastily, and he tramped back out to the front hall, leaving a pool of water at every step. Gramma went to the cupboard and got out a small plate. She cut a piece of pie for the professor, and then she went to get a mop. When the professor came back, he apologized for tracking up the floor, and Gramma said, "Ummm," which was her way of accepting an apology. Then everybody ate lemon meringue pie and listened to the professor as he complained about his car and life in general.

Later Grampa and Johnny got their coats and boots and hats on and went out to help the professor get his car unstuck. It was still snowing on Fillmore Street. Flakes came whirling down out of the dark sky. They looked black as they swept through the light of the streetlamp. Across the street was the professor's car. Its rear end was buried in a heap of snow. The situation looked hopeless, but Grampa reassured everybody. He said that he had once driven a Model T on muddy dirt roads in the springtime. And, said Grampa, if he could do that, he could get a car out of a miserable little bitty snowbank.

They set to work. The professor got into the car and started it. Grampa told him to rock it, and he and Johnny would push. The car rocked, and the wheels spun and whined. Spurts of snow flew up into the air. The professor had his car window open so he could give and get directions. Johnny could hear him cursing under his breath as the car lurched back and forth. At first nothing happened. The car just seemed to be digging itself deeper and deeper into a snowy rut. "Cramp the wheel over!" Grampa called. "Cramp it way over!" The professor cramped it over, and suddenly, with a jolt, the car shot forward, spraying wet snow all over Johnny and Grampa. The professor—who was not a very good driver, even under the best of conditions—pulled the car out into the middle of the street and did a U-turn, fish-tailing madly. The engine died, and he started it again. Finally he managed to nose the car over to the curb in front of Grampa's house. It was not a very good parking job. The rear end of the car was sticking out into the street. But the professor didn't care: he was disgusted and tired. He got out of the car, slammed the door, and stood there with his hands on his hips, glowering.

"Cars!" he snorted. "I *hate* them! Hate them, hate them, hate them! If I didn't have to have one to drive to work, I'd push this thing into the Merrimack River! So help me, I would!"

Grampa ambled slowly across the street, brushing snow off himself. "You know, Rod," he said slowly, "it would kinda help if you would put chains on your tires."

The professor looked startled, and then he waved his hand in an irritated way. "Oh, chains! Yes . . . hmm, yes, I suppose I *should* have thought of them! But I have so many things on my mind these days . . . hmmm . . . chains . . . yes. By the way, Henry, don't call me Rod. I hate to be called Rod. You know that."

"Sorry," said Grampa, shrugging apologetically. "I keep forgettin'."

"Think nothing of it," said the professor brusquely. "Can I come into your house and get something strong to drink? Some booze, I mean. It would make me feel better."

Johnny gasped. He had always had it drummed into his head when he was little that you never, never invited yourself into other people's houses. It was terribly impolite. But here was the professor—a college teacher and a respected member of the community—doing just that. And to top it all off, he was asking for liquor! Asking for it first, instead of waiting to be served. And Grampa didn't seem to mind at all. It seemed unfair, somehow.

Laughing and talking, the professor and Grampa

stomped through the snow and up the stairs to the porch. Johnny trailed along behind. When they got to the front door, they found Gramma blocking the doorway. She had a mop in her hand, and she looked grimly determined. She was not going to let the professor track up her rugs and floors a second time. He took the hint. Meekly, with downcast eyes, he shuffled over to the coat-tree, sat down on the boot box, and began peeling off his galoshes.

A few minutes later Johnny, Grampa, and the professor were all sitting around in the parlor, talking. Johnny had gotten a Coke from the refrigerator, and Grampa was drinking coffee. The professor had a water glass half full of whiskey in his hand. Gramma disapproved of liquor, so she was not present. She was upstairs in her bedroom, listening to the radio after saying her rosary.

"So, y'see, it wasn't such a big job after all," said Grampa amiably as he sipped from the steaming mug. "It only took us, oh, I'd say about twenty minutes, at the outside."

"Is that all?" grumbled the professor. He was trying hard to be grumpy, in spite of the cheerful company. "It seemed like *hours*. You know," he went on, wagging his finger at Grampa, "you know, Henry, in a hundred years people will think we were out of our ever-loving minds to spend so much of our valuable time taking care of automobiles. Think of it! Everybody on this block owns a two-ton hunk of metal that he has to feed gas and oil into, wash, and get fixed when it goes flooey. We spend half our lives thinking about cars! It's ridiculous, I tell you! Ree-*dick*-u-lous! Why . . ."

Suddenly the professor stopped talking. He had noticed something. On the floor next to the armchair that Johnny was sitting in was a pile of books. They were books on archeology that Johnny had taken out of the library recently: there were *Gods, Graves, and Scholars,* by C. W. Ceram, and *The Mountains of Pharaoh,* by Leonard Cottrell, and James Henry Breasted's *History of Egypt.* Egypt was Johnny's latest craze: he read everything he could about Egypt, and he was always combing the library for Egypt books that he hadn't read.

The professor looked at Johnny questioningly. "Are . . . are those books yours?" he asked. He said this as if he could scarcely believe that the answer might be yes.

Johnny did not see what was so unusual about reading books on Egypt. He was always reading books about something. "Yeah, they're mine," he said casually. "I mean . . . well, they're not really mine, they belong to the library. But I took 'em out to read, if that's what you mean."

"You took them out to read," the professor repeated in a wondering tone. "Do you have an assignment in school about Egypt? Is somebody *making* you read those books?"

Johnny grinned and shook his head. "Nope. I like to read."

The professor was astounded. He acted as if Johnny

had just told him that he was the pope, or the sultan of Zanzibar. "Good heavens!" he exclaimed. "You can read, and you *like* to read! Please excuse my amazement, but I have just come from visiting my sister's daughter, who lives up in New Hampshire. She has two children about your age, but they couldn't read their way through a book of cigarette papers. Which is scarcely odd, because their parents don't read anything except the phone book and the directions on spaghetti boxes. You like to *read*! Lord have mercy! Will wonders never cease!"

Johnny found that he was beginning to like the professor. He smiled happily and felt proud. Usually grown-ups were not in the least interested in Johnny's reading ability. If they noticed it at all, they said, "Oh, that's nice," in a polite sort of way. But what they really thought—as Johnny well knew—was that boys who liked reading as much as he did must be weird.

Johnny asked the professor some questions about mummies, and the professor answered them as well as he could. From mummies the conversation turned to ghosts, and the professor told about the haunting of the Borley Rectory in England and other spooky happenings that he had heard about. Johnny loved ghost stories. That was one of the reasons he listened to *The House of Mystery* and *The Hermit's Cave*. But, as he told the professor, he didn't actually believe in ghosts, not really. As far as Johnny was concerned, believing in ghosts was . . . well, it was like believing in Santa Claus, or the Easter Bunnny. It was for little kids, not for him.

"Oh, is that so?" said the professor, eyeing Johnny curiously. A faint half-smile curled the corners of his mouth. "Is that really so? It's kid stuff, is it? Well, my friend, you might be surprised someday. Do you know about the ghost of Father Baart that haunts the church you go to every Sunday? Do you? Hmmm?"

Johnny was really taken aback. He went to St. Michael's Catholic Church all the time, with his grandmother and grandfather. But he had never heard about any ghost.

The professor grinned. He could see that he had Johnny's attention. And then, without any further ado, he launched into his tale.

"Now then," he said, rubbing his hands, "it all began when . . . oh, by the way, Henry, I feel like some sort of cheap guzzler drinking this whiskey all by itself. Do you have anything to go with it? How about some of your wife's fudge? I think she makes wonderful fudge! Could I have some?"

Once again Johnny was amazed by the professor's crust. And, as before, Grampa didn't seem to mind. He went out to the kitchen and came back with a blue Willoware plate that held several thick squares of dark chocolaty fudge. Everybody took one, and as he munched the professor went on with his story.

"Father Remigius Baart," he began, "was the rector of St. Michael's Church way back in the 1880s. He was the one who had the church built—the church that's there now. And he hired a wandering artist—a mysterious character who showed up in Duston Heights one day—he hired him, as I say, to do the altarpiece in the church." The professor paused and stared thoughtfully out the window. "I often wonder about that man—the artist, I mean. He claimed that his name was Nemo, but *nemo* is Latin for 'no one.' Well, whatever his name really was, he was a talented wood-carver. All those saints and angels and prophets on the altar screen! I've never seen anything quite like it. But it seems that the wood-carver was more than just a wood-carver. The story is that he had dealings with the devil, that he diddled around with the black arts. The truth, I suppose, will never be known. After he finished the altar screen and got paid, this Nemo character left town and was never seen again. But people claim that before he left, he gave Father Baart something."

Johnny by this time was totally fascinated. He was sitting way forward on the edge of his seat. "What was it?" he asked. "What did this Nemo guy give to the priest?"

The professor stared at Johnny strangely. "Nobody knows. He may not have given him anything, but a lot of the older people in this town—your grandmother, for instance—will swear up and down that the artist gave Father Baart a talisman, or a book, or some sort of evil object that allowed him to do all kinds of nasty things, and may—in the end—have caused his own destruction."

The professor paused and grabbed another piece of fudge. He stuffed it in his mouth and chewed it slowly, savoring every chocolaty smidgin of it. The professor loved dramatic pauses. He felt that they added to his stories. Johnny squirmed impatiently in his seat. He wanted to hear more.

"Mmmm! Dee-*li*-cious fudge!" said the professor, smacking his lips. "Absolutely scrumptious! By the way, where was I? Ah, yes. Now, at this point you have to know what sort of man Father Baart was. He was not popular. He had a sharp tongue, and he used it often, and he had made quite a few enemies in the town of Duston Heights. If the people in the church had had their way, they would have got rid of him. They would have found a new rector. But only the bishop could fire him, and he didn't feel like it, so Father Baart stayed and made enemies. Well! A little while after the mysterious artist left town, funny things started to happen. Mr. Herman—he was a rich farmer in the area, and there was no love lost between him and Father Baart—Mr. Herman, I say, was standing looking up at the tower of the church one day—they were still building it at the time—and a carved stone, a big, heavy pinnacle that had just been put in place on top of the tower, fell off and hit Mr. Herman—killed him outright!"

Johnny wanted to say something, but the look on the professor's face told him he wasn't finished talking. So he waited.

The professor took another little sip of whiskey and another little nibble of fudge, and then he went on. "So Mr. Herman was dead. There were no workmen on the tower at the time, so nobody could be blamed. The coroner's verdict was 'accidental death.' Nothing to argue about—the stone was probably loose for some reason. But a few days later somebody else got eliminated. This time it was Mrs. Mumaw. She was another one of Father Baart's enemies. She had disagreed with him publicly, at parish meetings, and she had told him his qualities in no uncertain terms. And what happened to her? She got run down by a horse pulling a wagonload of barrels. One minute the horse was standing quietly in front of a store on Main Street; the next minute it was charging wild-eyed at Mrs. Mumaw, dragging the wagon, hell-bent for election, behind. Well, that was the end of *her*!" The professor paused and peered at Johnny over the tops of his glasses. "Now, then, my fine feathered friend," he said, "does anything occur to you? Hmmm? Does it?"

Johnny looked thoughtful. He saw what the professor was getting at. "It sounds kinda like . . . like Father Baart made those accidents happen. Like maybe he murdered those two people some way."

"You catch on fast," said the professor dryly. "Many of the people who were living in this town back then thought that Father Baart had murdered Mr. Herman and Mrs. Mumaw. But there was no way they could prove it. No way at all." The professor paused and sipped at his drink. "However," he went on, "however, and be that as it may, Father Baart got his comeuppance. He got it in spades!"

Johnny's eyes were wide. "What happened to him? Did the ghosts of the people he killed come back and get him?" Johnny had read some stories where things like that had happened.

The professor smiled mysteriously. "Nobody knows what happened to Father Baart," he said somberly. "One morning he didn't show up to say Mass in the church, and people got worried. His housekeeper and some other people went to the rectory and searched all the rooms, but he was gone. His clothes were still in the bedroom closet, and everything else was in its usual apple-pie order. But Baart was gone. The only clue left behind—if you want to call it a clue—was a note, found under a paperweight on his desk. The note was not written in Baart's handwriting—nobody knows who wrote it. To tell the truth, the note was not terribly helpful. It was simply a quotation from *Urne-Buriall*, which is an essay that was written long, long ago by an Englishman named Sir Thomas Browne. I like the essay—I like it a lot. And I've memorized parts of it. Let me see . . . I think I can quote for you the passage that was in the note."

The professor paused and closed his eyes. Then he smiled and nodded and opened his eyes again. "Ah. Ah, yes. I have it. This is the way it goes: 'The man of God lives longer without a Tomb than any by one, invisibly interred by Angels; and adjudged to obscurity, though not without some marks directing human discovery.' "

The professor paused again. He looked at Johnny. "There! Did you understand any of that?"

Johnny shook his head.

The professor sighed. "Well, it's a bit obscure, I must admit. The passage refers to Moses. According to the Bible, when Moses died, his body was carried away by angels and was buried secretly somewhere. Now, what that has to do with Father Baart's disappearance I don't know. But that was the message that was found on his desk after he vanished. He was never seen again . . . not *alive*, anyway."

Johnny looked puzzled. "Do you mean . . . did they find his body somewhere?"

The professor shook his head and smiled tantalizingly. "No. I didn't mean that. They never found his body. But he has been seen in St. Michael's Church, several times. Every now and then late on a winter night somebody will be sitting in the back of the church saying the rosary or praying. And then this person will feel a sudden chill and hear a funny noise. And they'll turn around, and there he'll be, big as life!"

Johnny's mouth dropped open. "Father Baart?"

The professor nodded. "The same. He was quite a striking-looking person—you'd never mistake him for anybody else. He was short and wore a black cloak, and he had a big head and a jutting chin and lots of grayish hair that he wore long. And an overhanging forehead, and a hawkish nose, and deep-set, burning eyes. So if you're ever in the church late at night, well . . ."

"Oh, for pity's sake!" said Grampa, cutting in. "Don't scare the poor kid to death! I'll never get him to go to church with his gramma on Wednesday nights if you carry on like that! By the way, I think it's a shame that a man like that, a priest and all, should have gone over to the devil. Servin' the powers of evil and darkness. Can you imagine?"

The professor twisted his mouth into a wry smile. "It's happened before," he said. "If you read your history, you'll find that some of the great medieval sorcerers were priests. Like Roger Bacon and Albertus Magnus. Of course, they stayed on the white magic side . . . most of the time. But if you fool around with magic, there must be a terrible temptation to call upon the powers of hell. After all, white magic can only do so much. It can't get revenge for you. It can't help you to wipe out an enemy. Only the bad guys can help you with that."

Silence fell. The story was over, and neither Johnny nor Grampa felt like asking any more questions. The professor gobbled the last piece of fudge, and then he announced that he had to go. It was getting late, and he had papers to correct before he went to bed. Johnny had homework to do, so he went out to the dining room table, turned on the light, and sat down to struggle with the square-root problems he had been given. The front door opened and closed. The professor was gone. Grampa went back to the parlor to get the plates and glasses. On his way to the kitchen he stopped by the table where Johnny was working.

"Some story, eh?" he said, chuckling. "That old so-and-so sure knows how to scare you, don't he?"

Johnny looked up. "You mean you don't think it's the truth, Grampa?"

Grampa looked thoughtful. "Well, I wouldn't go so far as to say that the old boy was feedin' you a line of bull, but . . . like I say, he loves good stories, and he sure knows how to tell 'em!"

Johnny felt disappointed. He was not nearly as skeptical as he thought he was. When he heard a good story, he always wanted to believe that it was true. "It . . . it *might* be true," he said weakly.

"Oh, sure," said Grampa with a humorous shrug of his shoulders. "It *might* be!" He chuckled and went on out to the kitchen with the dishes.

Johnny struggled a bit with his homework, but he found that his eyes kept closing. Oh, well. He could get up early tomorrow and do it before breakfast. Johnny closed his book and turned off the light. He went to the front door and rattled it, as he always did, and then he started up the steps. Halfway up he paused. There was a tiny square window there, and he liked to peer out of it. He watched the snow fall for a while. He imagined it falling on the cemetery, far away, where his mother lay buried. Sadness welled up in Johnny's heart. Tears sprang to his eyes. He wiped the tears away with his sleeve. Then he turned and climbed on up the stairs to bed.

CHAPTER TWO

Days passed. Weeks passed. Nothing very exciting happened to Johnny. He had the usual things to do, like snow shoveling, dish drying, and homework. Johnny went to St. Michael's School, a Catholic grade school in the town of Duston Heights. It was a two-story brick building with a slate roof and a pointed stone arch on the front. At St. Michael's, Johnny was taught by the Sisters of the Immaculate Heart of Mary. They wore navy-blue robes with black scapulars and black veils. The seventh-grade teacher was Sister Electa. She was nice, most of the time, but she really piled the homework on. Not that Johnny had a lot of trouble with homework. He was a real brain, and everybody at St. Michael's School knew it. Most of the other kids didn't mind that

Johnny was smart. They thought it was odd, but they didn't hold it against him. But there was one kid who was really jealous of Johnny. The kid was named Eddie Tompke.

Eddie was a seventh grader, like Johnny. He lived on a farm outside of town, and as everyone knows, farm work builds up your muscles. Eddie was strong, and he was good-looking. He thought that he owned the world, and he was ready to fight any kid who got in his way. Eddie had problems, though: He was not doing very well in school. His last report card had been all C's and D's, and as a result he had gotten a royal chewing-out from his father. So Eddie was mad a lot of the time now. He was mad at the world in general, but he was particularly mad at Johnny Dixon. Lately Johnny had begun to notice the way Eddie felt about him. Standing in line during lunch hour one day, he had happened to turn around, and he saw Eddie scowling at him. And later Johnny had been standing around on the playground, talking to another kid, and Eddie had walked by and kicked him in the shins for no reason at all. And now, whenever Johnny passed Eddie, Eddie would glower and say things like "I wish *I* was a brain!" or "It must be great to be a brown nose. Is that how you get those good grades, kid? Because you're the biggest brown nose in the school? Is that how you do it?"

All this had Johnny worried. He was short and he wore glasses and he was not very strong. Also he was in a new school, and he had not yet made any close friends.

And he had a very great fear of getting beat up. It was one of his really big fears, like his fear that someday he would step on a nail, get an infected puncture wound, and die of lockjaw. Johnny was always reading things in the paper about people who had gotten "beaten to a pulp" or "beaten beyond recognition," which meant that they had gotten smashed up so badly that no one could tell who they were. Stories like this hit Johnny right in the pit of his stomach. And he wondered, often, whether someday Eddie Tompke might get it into his head to beat him up.

One cold dark February day Johnny was standing under the big stone arch out in front of St. Michael's School. The school day was over. Everyone else had gone. As usual he was the last kid out of the building. He fiddled with his scarf and adjusted his stocking cap on his head. Johnny was a fussy kid—everything always had to be just so, or it was no good. Finally he was ready to go. Johnny peered out to his right. Oh, no. There was Eddie! He was standing on the corner, talking to some other kid. His back was to Johnny—he hadn't seen him yet. But he would when Johnny came that way, and he had to go that way to get home. Johnny peered quickly around the corner. A narrow alley ran between St. Michael's Church (which stood on the corner) and the school. If he moved fast, Johnny could zip down the alley and get out onto the street in any of three different ways. But for some reason Johnny decided that he would duck into the church. He could say a prayer for his mother and hang around till Eddie went away.

St. Michael's Church was a tall brick building with a brick steeple on the northeast corner. There were three big, pointed wooden doors at the front of the church. A flight of worn stone steps led up to each one. Johnny headed for the nearest door. It was a short dash, and he made it easily. Now he was tugging at the heavy iron ring. The door swung open. Johnny slipped inside, and the door closed behind him, *Clump!* Johnny heaved a sigh of relief. He had made it.

Johnny was standing in the vestibule, which is what the front hall of a church is called. He dipped his fingers in the holy water font, made the sign of the cross, and shoved open one of the inner doors. He was in the main body of the church now. Rows of wooden pews stretched away before him. Overhead arched the high vaulted ceiling. It was painted midnight blue and was powdered with little gold stars. At the far end of the nave was the Communion rail, and beyond it was the altar and the massive carved altarpiece. Johnny liked the old church. It was vast and gloomy and smelled of incense and candle wax. He loved the flickering red sanctuary lamp and the strange pictures on the stained-glass windows. The church was a place where he often went just to sit and get away from the world.

Johnny walked down the main aisle. His footsteps, though soft, seemed to echo from the high ceiling. When he got to the broad polished steps that led up to the Communion rail, Johnny stopped. With his arms folded over his chest he gazed up admiringly at the altarpiece that the mysterious Mr. Nemo had carved. It was quite a production. Over the altar table rose a three-decker wooden screen with lots of pointed niches in it. Each niche had an elaborately carved hood, and in the niches were wooden statues. The statues were painted all different colors, and gold paint had been used lavishly. The statues in the lower two levels were of saints. There were Saint Peter and Saint Paul and Saint Catherine and Saint Ursula and some nameless saints with swords and palms in their hands. At the top of the screen there were only three statues. These three were angels. One held a trumpet; one held a sword and shield; and one held a golden censer on a chain.

Johnny went on staring at the altar screen for a while. Then he went over to the iron vigil-light rack that stood near the confessional. He lit a candle for his mother, and then he walked down the side aisle and out into the vestibule again. Cautiously Johnny pushed the main door of the church open. He didn't open it far, just a crack. Darn! Eddie was still there!

Johnny let the door fall softly shut. Now what was he going to do? Gramma would be expecting him—he couldn't stay here forever. There was a back way out, but you had to go up into the sanctuary and out through the sacristy to get to it. And only Father Higgins and the altar boys and the sisters were allowed to go out that way. If Father Higgins caught him going through the sacristy, he would have a fit. Johnny stood, pondering, in the dark vestibule. He felt frustrated; he felt trapped. Then suddenly he had a very strange and interesting idea. He would go have a quick look in the basement.

Johnny grinned. He was a well-behaved kid most of the time, but he wasn't all *that* well behaved. Like most kids he enjoyed poking around in places that were forbidden. And he knew he was alone—there wasn't anybody in the church but him. Now was the time!

Quickly Johnny walked down to the far end of the vestibule. Now he was standing under the belfry. Overhead was a wooden ceiling with holes in it: the bell ropes hung through the holes. There was the dark, varnished wooden staircase that led up to the choir loft. And under the staircase, set in a paneled wall, was a narrow door with a black china knob. It led down to the basement. Johnny paused. He was thinking about the ghost of Father Baart. What if he appeared now? Or what if he suddenly materialized in the dark basement? Johnny shrugged and forced himself to smile. Hadn't Grampa told him that the professor's story was really a lot of hooey? Sure. There was nothing to worry about.

Johnny put his hand on the knob. He twisted, and the door opened easily. Mr. Famagusta, the janitor, was supposed to keep this door locked. But, as Johnny well knew, Mr. Famagusta was a rather careless man. Johnny put his foot on the first step, and then he pulled it back. He needed something . . . ah! There it was! The flashlight! Johnny had heard Mr. Famagusta say that there was no electric light in the church basement. And, sure enough, on a little dusty ledge near the door was a small and rather battered flashlight. Johnny picked it up, snapped it on, and started down.

The flight of creaky steps turned once at a wooden landing and went on down to a hard-packed dirt floor. Johnny played the flashlight beam around. Some rickety shelves had been built into the wall underneath the steps. He saw a silver censer that was so tarnished that it looked black. A grimy, cobwebbed box that said AD ALTARE DEI INCENSE. A headless plaster statue of some saint. A glass tumbler full of cassock buttons. A pipe wrench and a section of brass pipe, left—no doubt—by the careless Mr. Famagusta.

Johnny played the beam back into the darkness of the basement. He saw the brick pillars that held up the floor of the church. Beyond the first row of pillars was a stack of tabletops. Leaning against the stack was a raffle wheel, the kind they used for the turkey raffles at Thanksgiving time. And in the shadowy distance he could see the big sooty iron furnace that heated the church in the wintertime. Johnny sighed. The whole place was a lot less interesting than he had hoped it would be. He pointed the beam of the flashlight here and there. Without much interest he noticed a bookcase with warped, sagging shelves. The top shelf was empty, but the second shelf held a row of thick, black volumes. Johnny reached for one of the books, but he jerked his hand away with a disgusted cry. The book was crawling with little gray spiders.

Johnny closed his eyes and shuddered. He couldn't help it. He hated spiders, and the small gray ones were, to him, the most disgusting of all. A bad taste rose into Johnny's mouth, but he swallowed, and it went away. Johnny opened his eyes. He shone the flashlight at the book again. The spiders were gone! Well, now, that was odd—where had they gone to? Johnny looked at the floor. Nothing there. Then he pointed the flashlight at the wall behind the bookcase. It was a brick wall, and it was in pretty bad shape. The mortar looked powdery and loose, and the bricks were crumbling. In one place the mortar between two bricks had fallen out, and there was a hole. Maybe that was where the spiders had gone. Johnny went back to looking at the row of books. For some reason he was interested in the book that had had the spiders on it. He wanted to take it out and look at it. Three times he reached out his hand to touch it, and three times he jerked his hand back at the last minute. Finally, on the fourth try, his hand closed over the end of the grimy book. He pulled it out quickly and stepped back. Now he carried the book over to the stairs and laid it down on one of the lower steps.

Johnny played the flashlight over the cover of the book. The faint gold letters said ROMAN MISSAL. Now Johnny reached out in a gingerly way and took hold of the dog-eared cover. With a quick motion he flipped it back.

And then he gasped.

The inside of the book had been hollowed out. Only the outer part of each page was left. And in the hole that had been made were two things: a small rolled-up piece of yellowish paper tied with a faded red ribbon, and a strange little blue ceramic statue. The statue was shaped like an Egyptian mummy case. It had staring eyes and a tiny beaked nose and a smiling mouth and a scrolled goatee. The figure's arms were crossed over its breast in the Egyptian style. Apparently the mummy was supposed to be the mummy of a pharaoh, because it held in its hands the crook and the flail, the symbols of kingly power in ancient Egypt.

Johnny was utterly amazed. With the flashlight held steady in his left hand he reached into the hollow book with his right hand. He did this very cautiously, as if he expected something to bite him. But nothing did. He pulled out the little paper scroll and yanked at the rotting ribbon, which was tied in a bow knot. The ribbon came off, and Johnny held the paper up to the light. It had been rolled up for so long that it was permanently curled. Nevertheless Johnny could read the shaded, heavy, masculine script:

> Whoever removes these things from the church
> does so at his own peril. I abjure you by the living
> God not to endanger your immortal soul.
> *Vengeance is mine; I will repay, saith the Lord.*
> Remigius Baart

CHAPTER THREE

Johnny's eyes grew wide. He felt cold all over. Carefully, with a trembling hand, he put the scroll back in the hollowed book. He was about to close the lid when he heard a noise behind him, a rustling noise, like something moving about.

Johnny panicked. He didn't have time for making decisions; what he did was sudden and automatic. He lunged at the book, gathered it up in his arms, and stumbled madly up the steps. He never looked back to see what had made the noise. And when he got to the top of the stairs, Johnny slammed the door and leaned his body against it. He was panting and breathless, and when he looked at his hands, he saw that they were black with dust. The front of his parka was dirty too. And here was the book in his arms, and inside were the things that Father Baart had put into the book. It was all true, then, about Father Baart and the magical something that the mysterious wood-carver had given him. Or was it? Johnny felt that his brain was whirling. Nothing made any sense. He thought about what it said on the scroll. Should he put the book back? No. He was not going down into that basement again, not right away. Then should he drop the book and run? Slowly he walked toward the middle door of the church. He pushed it open and peeked out. Eddie had gone at last. There was no one around, no one at all. With the book clutched tight in his arms Johnny edged out through the half-open door. He paused for a second more, and then he hurried down the steps.

As he tramped along through the snowy streets with the book in his arms Johnny found that his mind was beginning to clear. He was thinking again. He thought about what Gramma would say if he came waltzing in the front door with this enormous black book. She would be upset about his dirty hands and his dirty parka, and she would certainly get nosy about the book. At the end of his own street Johnny stopped. He cut across a vacant lot and walked on down Marshland Avenue, which was the next street over. Then he stopped again in front of a big gray house that had a For Sale sign on it. This house was directly behind his own house. Johnny had used this sneaky shortcut before: down the driveway, over the bent wire fence, and into his own backyard. From there Johnny headed straight for the cellar door. It was an old-fashioned cellar entrance: two slanted wooden doors set up against the foundation of the house. These doors were never locked. Grampa was always going in and out this way, carrying papers to the incinerator or garbage to the garbage cans. Johnny glanced quickly up at the back windows of the house to see if anyone was looking out, and then he opened the doors. Quickly he raced down the steps and dumped the book in a dark corner. Then he raced back up the steps and closed the doors. Whistling softly, Johnny tramped up the snowy driveway and mounted the front steps. He took off his boots and stepped in the front door. He felt very pleased with himself—he had made it.

That night, after Gramma and Grampa had gone to bed, Johnny went down to the cellar and brought up his prize. He carried it to his bedroom, closed the door, and threw the bolt. After putting the book down carefully on the floor Johnny went to the closet and dug a soiled undershirt out of his laundry bag. He used the undershirt to wipe some of the soot and grime off the old book. Then he opened the cover and knelt there, admiring. He looked like a worshiper, and in fact that was how he felt. This was—Johnny felt sure—a sacred object, a magic object. He had no doubt that this was the very thing that the mysterious wood-carver had given to Father Baart. Johnny felt awestruck and also a little afraid. Should he even touch the statue? Well, he had already touched it, and nothing had happened to him. He had done something else too. He had disobeyed the grim command that Father Baart had written out: He had taken the statue out of the church. Johnny gazed at the little figure that smiled up at him, and he wondered if maybe he had done something foolish. He wanted to talk to somebody about the statue. But who could he talk to? Not Gramma—that was for sure. She would go through the roof if she knew that he had this thing. Grampa would be more understanding, but he would definitely not approve of stealing things from a church. So who could he talk to?

The professor! Of course!

Johnny grinned. Why hadn't he thought of the professor before? The professor was smart, and he knew about a lot of things. He probably knew about magic. And he was the one who had told Johnny the story of Father Baart in the first place. He would be very interested in Johnny's discovery. Furthermore Johnny did not think that the professor would tell on him. The professor was kind of a nut, and nutty people don't rat on you. Nice, friendly, ordinary next-door-neighbor types —they would rat on you and think nothing of it. But a nutty person never would.

Johnny closed the book up again and carried it to his closet. He put it down in the bottom and heaped old sweatshirts and bare blankets and copies of *Boys' Life* on top of it. Gramma wasn't nosy. She never poked into Johnny's private things. He figured his treasure would be safe there, for the time being.

Days passed. Johnny bided his time, waiting for a chance to go see the professor. The time came on a Saturday afternoon. Gramma and Grampa went down to the A&P to shop, and Johnny was left alone in the house. From the bay window in the front parlor he could see the professor's big gloomy gray stucco house. The professor's car was sitting in the driveway, so Johnny figured that he had to be home. He ran upstairs to his room and dug the black book out of his closet. In no time at all he was on the professor's doorstep with the book in his arms. Johnny set the book down on the doormat and pushed the doorbell button. He waited—no answer. Again he pushed the button, and again. Still nothing. Johnny shifted nervously from one foot to the other. What was the professor doing? Johnny fussed and fretted. He really wanted to talk to the professor, and he wanted to talk to him now. Finally he got so impatient that he took hold of the knob and turned it. The door was not locked —it flew right open.

Johnny stood and watched as the door swung back. Should he go in? It would certainly not be polite. But what if the professor had had a heart attack? Shouldn't he rush in and try to help him? Johnny decided that the professor needed him. He picked the book up, took a deep breath, and stepped over the threshold.

Straight down the long front hall he walked, and into the dining room. Nobody there. He peered into the kitchen. There was nobody there, either, but on the drainboard next to the sink lay a large hinged metal gadget. Johnny knew what it was—it was a jar wrench. You used them to get the lids off bottles and jars. Curious, Johnny moved closer. He peered into the sink and saw smashed pieces of glass, a jar lid, a lot of olives, and a pool of green brine. Johnny stared at this mess for a few minutes. Then—still holding the book carefully in his arms before him—he moved into the dining room. Now he began to hear muffled thudding and bumping noises. They seemed to be coming from upstairs. Johnny was becoming alarmed. He set the book down on the dining room table and galloped up the stairs. "Professor! Professor!" he called. No answer. Johnny ran down the hall and paused by the door of the room that the noises seemed to be coming from.

"Professor! Are you all right?"

A muffled answer came. "Yes, blast it, I'm *all right*! Half a minute and I'll be with you!"

Johnny waited, and presently the door of the room opened. There stood the professor, and he was quite a sight: He was wearing a baggy gray sweat shirt and gray sweat pants. His feet were bare, his hair was a mess, and he was not wearing his glasses. He blinked peevishly at Johnny.

"Yes? Yes? Who is it? I can't see a blasted thing without my glasses. And what are you doing here, anyway, whoever you are? This is a private home, you know. And if you're selling something, I'm not interested."

Johnny was bewildered by this crabby speech. "It's

. . . it's me, Professor. Johnny Dixon. I heard these noises, and I thought maybe you were being strangled or having a heart attack or something, so I came on up."

The professor's manner changed. He blinked some more, and then he smiled. His cheeks turned red, and Johnny saw that he was really quite embarrassed. "I'll . . . I'll be with you in a moment," the professor muttered. He turned and groped his way over to his desk. More groping, and he found his glasses. He put them on.

"Ah! Ah, yes, it *is* you, isn't it? And I'll bet you're wondering what I'm doing all dressed up like this, aren't you?"

"I . . . I was, kinda," said Johnny shyly.

The professor took Johnny by the arm and led him over to an open closet door. Johnny looked in. He saw that the walls and the floor of the closet were covered with padded gymnasium mats. Taped to the inside of the closet door was a hand-lettered sign that said:

TO FUSS IS HUMAN;
TO RANT, DIVINE!

"This is my fuss closet," the professor said casually. "As you know, I have a rotten temper. And I lost it, just a few minutes before you came in, because I could *not* get the lid off that bloody jar downstairs! So, I came up here—as I always do in such cases—and I put on these clothes and took off my glasses and went into my fuss closet, and I *fussed*! I cursed and yelled and pounded the walls and floor. And you know, I feel *much* better now.

Sweatier and tireder, perhaps, but better!" The professor heaved a deep, self-satisfied sigh and folded his arms. He smiled kindly at Johnny. "Now, then, what can I do for you? Hmmm?"

Johnny was so flabbergasted by the tale of the fuss closet that it took some effort to drag his mind back to what he wanted to talk about. "I . . . I found something, Professor," he began slowly. "I was . . . kind of pokin' around in the basement of the church, and I think I found the . . . the stuff that that wood-carver guy gave to Father Baart."

Now it was the professor's turn to be amazed. "Good God!" he exclaimed. "Are you *serious*? Do you really mean what you just said?"

Johnny nodded emphatically. "Uh-huh. It was all inside of a fake book. Do you wanta see it? It's downstairs. I brought it over so you could have a look at it."

The professor sighed and looked down at the clothes he was wearing. "Well," he said, chuckling, "I hardly feel professorial in this getup, but I would like to have a look at what you've found. Sure. Go get the stuff and bring it up, and meanwhile I'll get some shoes on. These floorboards are like ice."

A few minutes later the professor was sitting at his desk with the fake book open before him. Johnny stood behind the desk, next to the professor's chair. The expression on his face was anxious. The room they were in —the room with the fuss closet—was the professor's study. Along one wall was a bookcase made out of bricks and boards. It was full of paperback books. Stacked here and there on the floor were blue exam books with grades and comments scrawled in red ink on their covers. Framed diplomas with gold seals hung crookedly over the bookcase. And next to the desk, piled against it like a rampart, was a wild, disorderly heap of papers and notebooks. In the corner behind the desk stood a stuffed owl on a tall fluted wooden pillar. And on the owl's head, perched a little to one side, was a small Boston Red Sox baseball cap.

The Professor harrumphed and jiggled around in his chair. Johnny wanted him to get down to business, to start examining the figurine. But the professor liked to take his own time about things. He brushed eraser dust off the faded green blotter that lay on the desk. Then he reached into a drawer and took out an ashtray and a small, flat cardboard box. The box was black and on its lid was a splendid golden two-headed eagle. The lettering on the box said BALKAN SOBRANIE. The professor opened the box and peeled back two whispery layers of gold-leaf paper. Johnny saw in the box a row of black cigarettes with gold tips. As he watched in exasperation the professor searched in the drawers of his desk for matches. At last he found some. He lit a cigarette and took a deep drag. Then, finally, he reached out toward the cavity in the hollowed-out book.

First he took out the scroll. He unrolled it and read it. His face was absolutely expressionless—he might have been reading the want ads in the daily paper. The professor put the scroll back in the box. Carefully, using both hands, he lifted out the blue figurine.

Johnny was on pins and needles. He watched as the professor examined the thing, puffed on his cigarette, said "hmmm" several times, and pulled the floor lamp closer to his desk. Now the professor tilted the figurine up so he could look at its base. Johnny noticed—for the first time—that there was a small, faded brown-paper label on the base. The professor adjusted his glasses and peered closer. Then he let out a loud whoop of laughter. He set the figurine down, threw back his head, and roared.

"Hah! That's a good one!" exclaimed the professor, pounding his hand on the desk.

Johnny was startled and utterly bewildered. "What . . . what is?"

The professor giggled some more. Then he picked up the figurine and held it so Johnny could see the label. "Here, have a look! This is funny, it really is! See—right there. There it is!"

Johnny looked. There was printing on the faded brown label, old-fashioned Victorian ornamental printing. It said:

SOUVENIR
OF
CAIRO, ILLINOIS

CHAPTER FOUR

❧

Johnny felt crushed. He felt cheated and humiliated and angry. He had been so sure, so absolutely sure, that he had found a genuine bona fide Egyptian magic amulet. And now, to find out that the thing was a souvenir! A crummy, cheap, stupid souvenir! Johnny had souvenirs in his room. One was a small birchbark canoe that he had gotten when he visited Glen Ellis Falls in New Hampshire with his parents. And there was the old crusty bronze hand bell with a handle shaped like Father Junipero Serra, a priest who explored California in the eighteenth century. Johnny's uncle had gotten that in California, and he had given it to Johnny. And now . . .

Johnny gazed forlornly at the professor. "Are you

sure it's a souvenir?" he said weakly. "I mean, couldn't the label be a fake or something?"

The professor had stopped laughing. He saw now that Johnny was very disappointed, and he felt sympathetic. "I'm sorry, John," he said, shaking his head sadly. "But I'm afraid this is a real genuine souvenir and nothing more. I'm not an Egyptologist—my field is the Middle Ages. But this is just the kind of thing that a town like Cairo, Illinois, would peddle as a souvenir. They pronounce it *Kay*-ro, by the way. It's a town way down in the southern part of Illinois, and it happens to have the same name as the capital of modern-day Egypt. So somebody probably thought it was clever to make a souvenir that looked like an Egyptian ushabti."

"A what?" Johnny had never heard this strange word before.

The professor was astonished. He knew that Johnny read a lot, and so—unreasonably—he thought that Johnny ought to know all sorts of obscure things. "You don't—well, I never! All righty then—this is what a ushabti is." The professor paused and laid the figurine down on the desk. He stubbed out his cigarette, shoved his chair away from the desk, folded his hands in his lap, and stared dreamily up at the ceiling. "First," he said, "you ought to know that the ancient Egyptians thought the next world—the place you go when you die—would be a lot like this world. And so in the next world people would have work to do. Plowing and sowing, carrying water up from the river, making bricks out of clay—

stuff like that. Well, to the Egyptians it didn't seem right that the pharaoh would have to do work in the next world. It would be . . . well, it would sort of be like making the President of the United States polish his own car. So the Egyptians made these little dolls called *ushabti*, and they were supposed to do the work *for* the pharaoh in the next world. Sometimes they put whole armies of these ushabtis in the tombs with the pharaohs. They come in all shapes and sizes: sometimes they look like dolls, and sometimes they're just miniature mummies, like this one here. The guy who designed this souvenir must have seen a ushabti in a museum, and he must have copied it. But this is a souvenir and nothing else. I'm sorry to disappoint you, but I'm afraid that's the case."

As Johnny listened to what the professor was saying he found that he was struggling to find some way of proving that the figurine was really magic after all. Johnny was a stubborn kid about the things he believed. He did not give up easily. "But, Professor," he said plaintively, "what about Father Baart and the wood-carver and all that stuff? People always said that the wood-carver gave Father Baart something magic, didn't they? And there's that piece of paper there, with Father Baart's handwriting on it, isn't there? What about that?"

The professor turned to Johnny. There was a sheepish, sad look on his face. "I'm afraid, my boy," he said, "that I started all this business by telling you that ghost story. I'm terribly sorry—I deserve to be punched! The trouble with me is, I love to tell stories, and I like to make them seem as realistic as possible. Now, it is true that several people have claimed that they saw Father Baart's ghost in the church. And for all I know they may really think that they *did* see him. Personally I don't believe in ghosts, except when I'm telling ghost stories. As for this scroll here"—he tapped the paper with his finger—"it *is* Father Baart's handwriting—that much I can tell you. I used to be the official historian of St. Michael's Church, and so I know about things like that. But what does this prove? Not much. The whole business with the book, the figurine, and the warning note may have been Baart's idea of a joke. Or he may have been serious. He may have thought this silly statue was really enchanted. Who knows?"

Johnny hung his head. "Is it all a fake, then? The whole darned story? Did you make it all up?"

The professor shook his head vigorously. "Oh, goodness, no! Most of the details in the story I told were true. Mr. Herman and Mrs. Mumaw really did get killed, and Father Baart really did disappear. But the two deaths were just a coincidence, and I don't think there was anything supernatural about Baart's disappearance. Baart was insane, and he probably had some insane reason for wanting to disappear. As for the note that was found on his desk, he probably wrote it himself. It's easy enough to disguise your handwriting if you want to do that sort of thing."

The professor paused and flicked the ash off his cigarette. He gave Johnny a hangdog, guilty look. "I'm sorry to pull the rug out from under you this way, John," he said in a low voice. "Next time I'll think twice before I tell a ghost story. But *please* don't think that this blue doojigger is magic—it isn't!"

Johnny sighed. He wanted to be mad at the professor, but he just couldn't manage it. In spite of his lousy temper, in spite of his love of making up things, the professor was really a nice guy. Johnny could tell that, and he felt that he could forgive the old man for having told a few white lies.

At this point the professor glanced at his watch. He said that he had papers to grade and that he was going to have to chase Johnny out of the house.

"However," the professor added, grinning slyly, "I would like to issue an invitation: This evening, after dinner, how would you like to come over for a game of chess and a piece of chocolate cake? I play a superlative game of chess, and the cakes I make are also excellent. How about it? Are you interested?"

Johnny nodded and grinned. He loved to play chess, but right now he didn't have a partner. Grampa's game was checkers, and sometimes Johnny got very bored with it. And he was nuts about chocolate cake with chocolate frosting. So it was decided: Johnny would come back after dinner and have dessert. But before he went, he had one more question.

"What should I do about this stuff?" he said, pointing to the book and the two objects that lay inside it. "Do you think I should try and take it all back?"

The professor thought a bit. He drummed his fingers on the desk top, and he puffed at his black and gold cigarette. "I definitely think," he said at last, "that you should *not* take these things back. In the first place, if Father Higgins or Mr. Famagusta caught you in the basement of the church, there'd be hell to pay. And in the second place, it occurs to me that the blue figurine may be valuable. People collect things, you know. They collect salt shakers and medicine bottles and old flatirons and buttonhooks. The figurine is only a souvenir, but it's an *old* souvenir—sixty years old, or more. I think you should write to *Hobbies* magazine and find out if your doohickey is worth something. In the meantime, however, if I were you, I'd keep the thing hidden. If your Gramma sees it, she'll ask where it came from, and then where would you be? Just take it back and put it in your closet. First, though, you'd better make sure the coast is clear. Come on. I'll go down with you and check."

Johnny took the book in his arms and followed the professor downstairs. At the front door they stopped, and the professor peered cautiously out.

"Good!" he said, nodding. "They're not back yet. You'd better get while the getting is good. Bon voyage! And don't forget about our chocolate cake date tonight!"

"I won't," said Johnny, grinning. "G'bye!"

While the professor held the door for him Johnny raced across the street. Into the house he went, and up the stairs to his room. Once again he put the old black book in the bottom of his closet. Again he piled stuff on top of it. Then he closed the closet door and went across the hall to wash his hands, which were dirty from handling the book.

That evening at dinner, just as Gramma was about to serve dessert, Johnny announced that he had been invited over to the professor's house for cake and a chess game. He announced this shyly and hesitantly, because he didn't know what Gramma's reaction would be. Grampa was a pretty easygoing sort—he usually let Johnny do what he wanted to do. But Gramma was more strict, and she didn't like the professor much. Furthermore she was proud of her desserts—Johnny didn't want to hurt her feelings or make her angry.

But all Gramma said was "Humph! I guess it's all right." And she added, in a disparaging tone, "I didn't know he baked cakes." Gramma had lived across the street from Professor Childermass for twenty years, but there were a lot of things she didn't know about him.

Johnny excused himself and went across the street. He had a great time that evening. The professor was a crafty and merciless chess player. He was every bit as good as Johnny was, and maybe even a bit better. As for the cake . . . well, Johnny had theories about chocolate cake. He felt that the cake part of the cake was just an interruption between the layers of frosting. As it turned out, the professor's opinions about cake were similar to Johnny's. The cakes he served had three or four thin layers, and the rest was a huge amount of good, dark, thick fudgy frosting. And he served second helpings too.

Around ten o'clock that night Johnny said good-bye to the professor and started across the street toward his house. He paused on the curb for a minute or two to look around. It was a beautiful cold winter night. Icicles hung from all the houses, and they glimmered gray in the moonlight. Snowdrifts lay everywhere. In the street were ridges of ice, knotted and iron-hard. Johnny blew out his cloudy breath and felt contented. He had made a new friend, he was stuffed with chocolate cake, and he had won one of the three chess games they had played. Once more he looked around, and then he stepped forward into the street. As he stepped he happened to glance to his left, and he stopped dead.

There was somebody standing across the street, watching him.

Johnny stared. Who was it? He couldn't tell. All he could see was a short, stocky figure standing in front of Mrs. Kovacs's house.

"Hi!" called Johnny, waving.

No answer. The figure did not move.

Oh, well, thought Johnny, *it's probably Mr. Swartout.* Mr. Swartout was a creepy little man who lived at the end of the street. He never said anything to anybody —wouldn't give you the time if you asked him for it.

Shrugging, Johnny walked straight on across the street and into his house. Later, upstairs, when he was in his pajamas and getting ready to climb into bed, Johnny looked out the window. His bedroom was at the front of the house. From it you could get a good view of the whole length of Fillmore Street. He looked toward the place where the figure had been standing, but there was no one there. For some reason Johnny felt relieved. Then he peeked at the moon, which was silvering the shingles of the professor's house. Johnny yawned and climbed into bed, and very soon he was asleep.

CHAPTER FIVE

In the weeks that followed, Johnny and the professor
became friends. It was an odd kind of friendship, the old
man and the twelve-year-old boy. But the friendship
worked. Johnny was a shy kid. He did not feel at home
with very many people. But he felt comfortable talking
with the professor. At chess they were pretty evenly
matched: Johnny won about half the games they played.
As for the professor's famous temper . . . well, he didn't
use it around Johnny. He crabbed now and then, but
he crabbed in a humorous and kidding way, so that
Johnny always knew he was not being serious. Gramma
—as you might guess—did not know what to make of
the friendship that had developed between these two.
She herself did not care much for the professor's com-

pany, but she didn't have anything serious against him, so she just sighed and shook her head and said many times that it takes all kinds to make a world.

The blue figurine stayed in its box in Johnny's closet. One afternoon when he was on his way home from school, Johnny took a detour and stopped in at the library. He went to the reading room and picked up a copy of *Hobbies* magazine. As the professor had said, it was a magazine for antique collectors. It was full of information about mechanical banks and oil lamps and bisque figurines and Toby jugs and Simon Willard clocks. And on one page there was a question and answer column. Johnny sat down and copied the address of the magazine into a notebook he was carrying. Later, when he was back at home, he went up to his room and got out his Royal portable typewriter. He set it up on his bed, and kneeling in front of it, he pecked out a note:

Dear Sirs:

I own a blue statue shaped like an Egyptian mummy. It is old and the label on the bottom says SOUVENIR OF CAIRO, ILLINOIS. I wonder if this statue is valuable.

Sincerely,
John Dixon
23 Fillmore St.
Duston Heights, Mass.

P.S.: Do not send a reply to my home. I will go to the library in the coming months to read your magazine and see if you have answered my query.

Johnny folded this note up neatly, put it in an envelope, and printed the *Hobbies* magazine address on the outside. He slapped on a stamp and put the letter in his briefcase, and the next day, on his way to school, he dropped the letter into a mailbox. And he thought about how nice it would be if the blue gizmo turned out to be worth fifty thousand dollars or something like that.

March was a wintry month in Massachusetts that year. Sea gales battered the town, and the snow stayed on the ground. Life went on in its usual routine for Johnny, for a while. But in the middle of March some rather odd things started to happen.

First there was the problem of the spiders. One day Johnny came home from school and found Gramma down on her knees on the parlor floor. She had a spray gun in her hands, and she was squirting insect spray along the baseboard. She looked upset.

"Hi, Gramma!" said Johnny. He threw his books onto the couch and walked over to get a closer look at what his grandmother was doing. "Whatcha doin', huh?"

Gramma glowered. She hated stupid questions. "What does it *look* like I'm doin', huh? I'm sprayin' away like crazy with this Black Flag insect stuff, on account of the house is full of spiders! *Spiders!* Can you imagine it, in the middle of winter?"

Johnny wanted to point out that it was not exactly the middle of winter but more like the end of it. But Gramma didn't like being corrected, so he said nothing.

He watched for a few minutes as she shuffled along on her knees, spraying as she went.

"I haven't seen any spiders," said Johnny after a while. "What kind are they?"

"Those rotten little gray ones," Gramma grumbled. "And if you haven't seen 'em, you must be goin' blind! Go out in the kitchen and have yourself a look. You'll be lucky if they don't carry you away with 'em. Spiders in winter! Lord! Where do you suppose they can be living?"

Johnny went out to the kitchen and looked. Sure enough, scooting here and there over the floor were small gray spiders. They were like the spiders he had seen crawling over the black book. Johnny felt an odd, queasy stirring of fear in his stomach. Quickly he told himself that he should not let his imagination run wild. These were just spiders and nothing more. And to prove this to himself he put out his foot and crushed one.

The spider invasion lasted several days. Then, mysteriously, they disappeared. Gramma was convinced the Black Flag spray had done its work. Johnny was not so sure.

One windy night toward the end of March Johnny went to the movies by himself. He went to see a spooky show called *The Ghost Returns*. By the time he got out of the theater, he was in a pretty nervous state. And as he made his way along the dark deserted streets toward home he began to get the feeling that someone was following him.

This is a maddening and frightening feeling, as everyone knows. Johnny kept telling himself that it was all in his mind, but still, as he walked from streetlight to streetlight, he found his fear growing. Once or twice he stopped suddenly and spun quickly around, but there was never anyone there.

When he got home, Johnny was somewhat taken aback to find that the house was dark. A note was taped to the window of the front door:

> *Gone next door to visit.*
> *Home later. Key under mat.*
> *Gramma and Grampa*

Johnny got out the key and let himself in. He was determined to shake off the nervous, frightened feeling that had come over him. First he turned on some lights. Then he marched straight out to the kitchen and got the pimiento-flavored cream cheese and the crackers. Then he went to the parlor, planted himself in the bristly brown chair, turned on the radio, and sat back to listen and munch. It wasn't a spooky show. It was *Camel Caravan*, a musical program that did the hit tunes of the week. Vaughn Monroe was on it, and some other singers that Johnny liked. Nevertheless, as he listened Johnny found his nervousness returning. He kept glancing toward the dark doorway of the room, but the doorway was always empty.

At ten o'clock Gramma and Grampa came home, and Johnny was very glad to see them. Gramma went straight up to bed. Grampa hung around downstairs to talk with Johnny for a while. But he was pretty pooped, so he did not stay very long. After a few minutes he too went to bed, and Johnny decided that it was pretty lonely sitting around downstairs. Wearily he climbed the steps. He washed up and brushed his teeth and put on his pajamas. Then he jumped into bed and pulled up the covers. Almost immediately he went to sleep. And he had a very odd dream.

He dreamed that he was back in Riverhead, walking down Main Street late at night. He was headed for the United Cigar Store. In real life Johnny had gone to the United Cigar Store many, many times. He had bought his first deck of Bicycle playing cards there, and he had picked up other things too. Odd trinkets like a ball-and-cup magic trick, a Chinese puzzle, a dribble glass, a joy buzzer. Now, in the dream, he was going to the United Cigar Store again, though he really didn't know why. He passed the Sunoco station, and then he was there. But what had happened to the store? Over the big red-and-white United Cigar sign a weathered wooden slab had been hung. The letters on the slab said:

R. BAART · ANTIQUES AND CURIOS
In the midst of life, we are in death.

Johnny looked up at the sign. It wasn't the sort of sign you usually saw, even on antique stores. But there was a light on inside, and for some reason Johnny wanted very much to go in. As he started up the steps he glanced at one of the display windows and noticed that the pipes and fishing reels and Kodak cameras were gone. Instead the bottom part of the window was full of grayish sand, and from the sand little blue mummy figurines stuck out. Each one had a grinning skull for a face.

Johnny opened the door and went in. The shop was dusty and disorderly. Gray spiders scurried across the floor. There was a heap of broken furniture in the back, and the only light came from a bare bulb that hung from a frayed black cord. There was a counter, with a display case below, but the windows of the display case were so flyspecked and dirty that Johnny couldn't see what was inside. Behind the counter stood the proprietor of the shop. She was an old lady, in a shapeless gray sack of a dress. She wore a large green eyeshade that covered the top half of her face.

"Can I help you, young man?" The voice was horrible and croaking.

Johnny knew that the old woman was really Father Baart, but for some reason he was not afraid. He said calmly, "I have come here to search for the answer to the mysteries of life."

The old woman grinned—Johnny could see her wrinkled mouth and strong, jutting chin below the shade. "Come around behind the counter, then," she barked. "Step this way, step right this way. . . ."

Johnny moved around behind the counter, and he saw

—to his horror—that the old woman was standing in an open grave. Behind her was a gravestone, and all around was long, matted grass. Johnny tried to turn and run, but his legs were like lead. The old woman had hold of his hand now, and she was pulling him down. He struggled. He planted his feet and tried to resist, but the old woman's grip was like an iron vise. The harder Johnny pulled, the closer he got to the grave. His feet were sliding, inch by inch, to the brink. And now he saw that the woman's face was a skull, a horrible grinning skull covered with black crisscrossed strands of spider web. Johnny was screaming, but he couldn't hear any sound. And now he was plunging down, down . . .

With a sudden jolt Johnny woke up. He was trembling all over. Was there anyone in the room? No, no one that he could see. The room was dark and quiet. From far away came the steady rattling roar of a freight train that was passing through the town. Johnny lay down and pulled the covers up over himself. But it was a long time before he could get to sleep again.

The next morning at breakfast Johnny was unusually thoughtful. Also his appetite was gone. He only ate a few spoonfuls of Gramma's delicious oatmeal (served with brown sugar, maple syrup, and raisins). Gramma asked him if he had something on his mind, and, lying, he said no. He just couldn't tell her, because he was thinking about the blue figurine. How would she feel if she knew he had swiped that gizmo from the church? Johnny had a pretty good idea of how she would feel. So he said nothing.

The school day passed in its usual way, except that Johnny was in a fog. He was usually quite alert and raised his hand a lot, but not today. In fact he got bawled out a couple of times by Sister Electa because he was not paying attention. Johnny was thinking about the spooky things that had happened to him lately. He was wondering if there was any connection between them and the blue figurine. He could not get Father Baart's grim warning out of his mind: *Whoever removes these things from the church does so at his own peril. I abjure you by the living God not to endanger your immortal soul. Vengeance is mine; I will repay, saith the Lord.* Was this warning just craziness, or was there something more to it? By the time school was over for the day, Johnny had made up his mind: He would have to see the professor about all this.

That evening, after dinner, Johnny went across the street to see his friend. He had called the professor up, and the professor had said sure, come ahead, he would be up in the bathroom sailing boats in the tub! Johnny did not know what to think of this, but he had learned to expect the unexpected from Professor Childermass. When he arrived at the door of the professor's bathroom, he found the old man kneeling beside the tub. He was wearing a rubber waterproof apron, and the sleeves of his shirt were rolled up. The tub was half full of water, and in it floated a fleet of little wooden boats. They were galleys, with matchstick oars and little triangular sails. Little paper flags fluttered from the sterns of the ships. Half of the flags were red and gold and had coats of arms on them. The other half were green and had gold crescents. The professor explained that he was re-enacting the Battle of Lepanto, which had taken place in 1571. In it the Christian ships led by Don John of Austria had defeated the ships of the Turks. With a little book open in his left hand and a stick held in his right the professor moved the ships around. When a ship got taken or sunk, the professor would reach in and lift it out of the water and put it on a shelf over the tub. Next to the tub was a blackboard where the professor kept score. The scoreboard looked like this:

Christians	Turks
THH II	III

"Now then," said the professor as he pushed two boats together, "what did you want to see me about?"

Johnny told him. He explained about the spiders and the feeling of being followed that he had had the other night, and about the dream. The professor listened thoughtfully while Johnny talked, but he did not seem particularly worried.

"Is that all?" said the professor when Johnny was through. "I mean, is that all that's got you worried?"

Johnny felt offended. Here he was trying to tell the

professor his troubles, and what he was getting in response was *Ho, hum, is that all?* "I . . . I thought you'd
tell me what to do," said Johnny in an offended voice.

Immediately the professor saw that he had hurt
Johnny's feelings. He hadn't meant to. Now he heaved
a deep, dispirited sigh. He stood up and started untying
the strings of his apron. "Look, John," he said slowly,
"I am not trying to make light of your worries. But I do
think this whole business is in your mind. Spiders can
find places to live and hatch their eggs in an old house
even in wintertime. As for your dream and your feeling
that you were followed . . . well, the power of sugges-
tion is pretty strong. You heard my ghost story—which,
by the way, I wish I had never, *ever* told you—and then
you found that dratted hunk of blue crockery. You've
got Father Baart and ghosts on the brain, my boy, and
that's why you've got the heebie-jeebies these days. And
do you know what I suggest as a cure? Hmmm?"

Johnny shook his head. "I dunno, Professor. What?"

The professor paused dramatically. He folded up his
apron and put it away in the bathroom closet. Then he
turned back to Johnny, rubbing his hands and grinning
hugely. "I would suggest," he said, "that you let me beat
the holy bejesus out of you in a chess game or two, and
that you then eat a huge, glutty, calorie-filled hunk of
my delectable prune cake, with creamy smooth chocolate frosting, and whipped cream on top. How's that for
a prescription? Eh?"

Johnny liked the idea. His little visit to the professor turned into a long and enjoyable—and filling—stay. When he went home that evening, he felt that maybe the professor was right after all. The whole business was just his imagination working overtime.

A month passed. Windy March turned into sloppy wet April, and—much to Gramma's annoyance—the spiders came back to 23 Fillmore Street. On the other hand the spooky feelings and dreams that had been bothering Johnny went away. And one evening, when he was down at the library, Johnny picked up the new April issue of *Hobbies* and saw that his question had been answered. This was the answer:

> We have consulted antique dealers in the city of Cairo, Illinois, and we have discovered that mummy-shaped souvenir figures were sold in that city late in the nineteenth century. They were made in three colors, gold, blue, and red, and they were manufactured by Mound City Novelties of St. Louis, Missouri. We are informed that such an object, in good condition, would be worth about $25 today.

Johnny closed the magazine and shook his head. Twenty-five dollars! Phooey. So much for his wonderful dream of getting rich in a hurry. But at least now he knew that the figurine was not some mysterious talisman from ancient Egypt. It was what the professor had said it was. Johnny felt very relieved, and once again he scolded himself for letting his imagination work overtime.

Toward the end of April St. Michael's School had its yearly paper drive. At St. Michael's it was turned into a big contest, the east side of the school against the west side. Sister Electa made up a song set to the music of "The Sidewalks of New York," and all the kids sang it in class:

> East Side, West Side,
> Which is going to win?
> We're looking for the paper
> In cellar, barn, and bin,
> Boys and girls together
> Working one and all,
> Bringing loads of paper
> From the sidewalks of our town!

Every day for three days the students of St. Michael's School were let out of class in the afternoon so they could go hunt for wastepaper. They went everywhere looking for it. Some kids went from house to house. Others—the cleverer ones—had aunts and uncles who had been saving newspapers for them all year. Now they gleefully lugged the bales in, tied up nice and neat. For the kids it was like a holiday. And it was a contest too— each side was fighting hard to win.

On the last day of the paper drive Johnny and a lot of other kids were over at the Parish Hall, working hard. The Parish Hall was a long red brick building that stood just to the west of the school. This was where the Friday-night bingo games were held. At paper drive time all the folding chairs and tables were stacked over on one side of the hall, and the bundles of tied newspapers lay in big heaps. Kids swarmed everywhere, and everybody was supposed to have something to do: Some kids tied loose paper into bundles, others counted the bundles, and still others helped unload paper from the flatbed trucks that backed up to the open freight door. Everybody worked, and everybody seemed to enjoy working. It was such a treat to be doing something besides school-work for a change!

On into the late afternoon Johnny toiled. He got paper cuts and twine burns on his fingers, and his shirt was soaked with sweat, but it didn't matter. He was working to help the east side of St. Michael's School win. Johnny was weary but happy. At last he felt like he belonged at St. Michael's School.

Around three thirty the Parish Hall began to empty out. Kids started to go home in ones and twos and threes. Johnny was still busy tying bundles. Then he heard somebody cough over his head. He looked up and saw that it was Sister Correda. Sister Correda was the first- and second-grade teacher. She was nice, but she was kind of scatterbrained. She was always forgetting where she left things.

"Uh . . . John?" she said in her hesitant way. Sister Correda always acted apologetic when she was about to ask a favor of somebody.

"Yes, Sister?"

"Would you please go over to the school and get my watch for me? I must have left it on the desk in my classroom."

"Sure, Sister. I'll be right back."

Johnny went out the door into the afternoon sunlight. He crossed a corner of the playground and climbed the concrete steps that led to the back door of the school. Now he was inside again, in the cool gloom of the building, which always smelled of varnish and chalk dust and library paste. Johnny went straight to the first-grade room. He opened the door and peered inside. There on the teacher's desk lay Sister Correda's watch. It was a silver-plated pocket watch, with a long braided piece of leather attached to it. And standing next to the desk with his hand reaching out toward the watch was Eddie Tompke.

As soon as Eddie saw Johnny, he jerked his hand back. Then he grinned nastily.

"Hello, Brown Nose," he said. "You're just in time. I was gonna take this watch over to Sister What's Her Name. Now you can save me a trip."

Johnny stood dead still, staring at Eddie. *I bet you were gonna take the watch over to Sister*, thought Johnny. *I just bet you were.*

Eddie glared right back at Johnny. His eyes were mean and hard. " 'Smatter, Brown Nose? Doncha believe me? Think I'm lyin' to ya? Huh?"

Johnny didn't know what to say. He was scared of Eddie, but he stood his ground. He wasn't going to run away. "You're not s'posed to be in here," he said in a strained, nervous voice. "If the sisters find out—"

"Well, the sisters won't find out unless you tell 'em, will they, Brown Nose? C'mon and get the watch. You scared to come and get it?"

Johnny felt the muscles in his stomach tighten. He wanted to turn and run. But he forced himself to walk forward to the desk. Now he was standing face-to-face with Eddie. For a second Johnny thought that he would have to fight Eddie to get the watch. But Eddie pulled his hand back as Johnny approached.

"Brown noses always run errands for the sisters, don't they?" said Eddie in a hateful, crooning voice. "That's how they get their good grades. Everybody ought to know that."

At this something inside Johnny snapped. Eddie was bigger and stronger than he was, but he just had to say something. Johnny looked at Eddie, and their eyes met. "I'm not a brown nose," he said evenly. "I just do my work."

For some reason this remark really seemed to make Eddie angry. Quick as a flash he reached out and grabbed Johnny's hand. With his other hand Eddie picked up something that lay on the desk. It was a kid's pair of scissors. Eddie reached out and clamped the scissors around the index finger of Johhny's hand. The finger was caught in the part of the scissors just above the rivet that held the two blades together. Eddie squeezed. It felt awful— it was like being tortured. Johnny bit his lip to keep from yelling. He didn't want to give Eddie the satisfaction of hearing him scream.

Eddie kept squeezing. Tears were in Johnny's eyes. Weakly he tried to shove Eddie away. At last Eddie let go. He dropped the scissors on the desk and said, "See you 'round, Brown Nose." Then he turned on his heel and left.

Johnny stood at the desk. He was crying and clutching his injured finger. It burned, it stung. Slowly the hurt began to go away. Johnny took off his glasses and wiped his eyes with his handkerchief. Then he put the glasses back on again and picked up the watch. Sister Correda would be wondering why it had taken him so long. He wanted to tell her what had happened, but he knew he wouldn't tell on Eddie. That was for tattle-taling babies, not for him.

Johnny went back to the Parish Hall and gave Sister Correda her watch. As soon as she saw him she knew something had happened. His face was red and streaked with tears, and he was sniffling.

Sister Correda was the flustery type, and she immediately got upset. "Good grief, John!" she exclaimed. "What . . . what happened to you?"

Johnny had a powerful urge to tell on Eddie, but he resisted. "I . . . I caught my hand in the door to your room," he said. And as proof he held up his sore and reddened finger.

Sister Correda was properly sympathetic. She took Johnny over to the sisters' house and put Unguentine on his finger. She gave him a glass of milk and a couple of Oreo cookies, and then she told him that he probably ought to quit working and go home. He wouldn't be able to tie up any bundles with his sore finger, and anyway it was about time to call it quits for the day.

"Besides, it looks as if your side has won," said Sister Correda, smiling. "That ought to make you feel good. And thank you for all the work you did. You're a real trouper—you never give up!"

Compliments alway made Johnny feel shy. "It was a lotta fun," he said, staring at the tablecloth.

Johnny talked a bit more with Sister Correda, and then he set out for home. At first as he walked along he felt good. His finger wasn't hurting much anymore. And he was very, very proud that his side had won the paper drive. But slowly the good feeling began to die away, and black anger took its place. Who did Eddie think he was, anyway? And what had he, Johnny, ever done to him? Nothing. Nothing except get good grades in school. And for this Eddie hated him. Well, right now Johnny was hating him back. He wanted to strangle Eddie, he wanted to murder him. In his mind's eye he saw himself pushing Eddie in front of cars, or beating him bloody in a boxing match. By the time Johnny got home, he was fairly tingling with hatred of Eddie.

Straight in the front door Johnny marched. Straight in the door and up the stairs to his room. He slammed the door of his room and threw the bolt. And then he did a very strange thing. He went to the closet, opened the door, and knelt down. Carefully he removed the sweat shirts and blankets and copies of *Boys' Life* that were piled on top of the black book. He opened the cover and took out the blue figurine. Then he clenched the thing tight in his hands and yelled at the top of his voice, *"I hope he breaks his goddam neck!"*

Johnny was silent. His face felt flushed, and he was breathing hard, and his heart was going like a trip-hammer. He felt scared. Scared of himself, scared of his anger, scared of what he had just said. And why was he holding the figurine? He had no idea why—no idea in the world.

With trembling hands Johnny put the figurine back in the book. He closed the worn, dog-eared cover, and he was about to start piling blankets on when he heard a knock at the door. Hastily Johnny threw stuff on top of the book. He got up and closed the closet door. Then he went to the door of his room and opened it. There stood Gramma. Her arms were folded, and she looked mad.

"John Dixon," she said severely, "I would like to know who gave you the right to come tearin' in here the way you did just now. When I heard your door slam, I thought the house was comin' down on top o' me! What's the matter with you, anyway?"

Johnny looked remorseful and stared at the floor. "Aw, I got in a fight with Eddie Tompke," he muttered. "He hurt my finger, and I got real mad. That's all."

Gramma looked a little less grim when she heard about Johnny's finger. "I know those Tompkes," she said, nodding meaningfully. "They're a mean bunch, all of 'em. Old Jack Tompke, he belonged to the Ku Klux Klan. Did you know that?"

Johnny said no, he didn't know that.

"Well, he did. Could I have a look at your finger?"

Johnny held out his hand. Gramma winced and made a *tsk-tsk* sound. "How'd he do *that* to you?" she asked.

"He caught it in a pair of scissors."

Gramma made more clucking sounds and shook her head. "Well, like I said, they're a mean bunch. Come on downstairs, and I'll put some witch hazel on that. It'll make it feel better."

So Johnny went downstairs with Gramma, and for the second time that afternoon he got his finger doctored. As Gramma fussed over him she went on about the Tompkes and their relations, the Tadmans and the Sweets and the Schemanskes. Gramma was like that. She had lived in Duston Heights all her life, and she knew everything about everybody. Usually this kind of thing bored Johnny, but right now he was happy that Gramma had the Tompkes to think about. It would make her forget about this door-slamming.

Later Johnny did some KP work in the kitchen for Gramma. He set the table for dinner, and he washed the celery, and he peeled some potatoes. But as he worked shapeless dark fears came crowding into his mind. Had he done something awful by grabbing the figurine and saying what he had said? If the professor knew about his fears, he would laugh and say that Johnny was letting his imagination run hog-wild. And it was certainly true that the figurine was just a souvenir and nothing more. The stories about Father Baart were just stories—that was also true, beyond doubt.

All the same Johnny was worried.

CHAPTER SIX

The next morning after breakfast Johnny went off to school as usual. At St. Michael's the school day always started with Mass in the church at eight. On this particular morning, as Johnny saw the great gloomy brick church looming up before him he felt a tightening in his gut. There was something he wanted to know—or rather there was something he was afraid of finding out. Up the worn steps and into the church he went. He paused in the vestibule to dip his fingers in the holy water font and make the sign of the cross. Then he pushed open the inner doors and walked down the aisle. The seventh graders always sat in the third and fourth pews back from the front, on the left side of the main aisle. When

Johnny reached the end of his pew, he genuflected and then started in.

Then he stopped. He stared, and his blood ran cold.

At the far end of the pew sat Eddie Tompke. His right arm was in a cast, and the cast was in a sling. Eddie had broken his arm.

Johnny stood dead still. His mouth hung slightly open, and he went on staring. Finally Eddie noticed him. He turned and scowled. He looked as if he wanted to say something nasty, but you weren't allowed to talk in church, and Sister Electa was sitting in the row behind.

"Hey, Dixon," somebody whispered. "Move it!"

Johnny came to himself with a jolt. He realized that he was blocking the entrance to the pew. He muttered " 'Scuse me" and sidled on down the pew till he was sitting next to Eddie. Johnny had barely gotten seated when the sanctuary bell tingled, and the priest and the altar boys came out of the little door to the right of the altar. The morning Mass had begun. Throughout the service Johnny stood and knelt and said prayers along with everyone else. But his mind was not on his prayers. He was thinking of something else. Yesterday he had held the blue figurine in his hands, and he had wished that Eddie would break his neck. He hadn't broken his neck, but he had broken his arm. Was it a coincidence? Johnny didn't think so. He felt scared, and he felt terribly guilty. He felt like he was sitting next to the body of somebody he had murdered. He wanted to turn to Eddie and say "I'm sorry," but Eddie would not have understood what he was talking about. And Johnny would have gotten bawled out for talking in church.

Mass was over, and the kids filed out of the church two by two. Soon Johnny was seated at his desk in the second-floor classroom. Sister Electa announced that the east side had won the paper drive. Everybody whooped and cheered. Johnny tried to cheer, but what came out was kind of weak. Yesterday he would have been thrilled. But now a dark fear filled his mind, and he could not get rid of it.

Johnny went through the rest of the day mechanically, like a robot. He did his arithmetic and religion and history lessons, but his mind was in a fog. Out of the fog thoughts came floating: he told himself that he was getting upset over nothing. It was all just a coincidence. Eddie's broken arm had nothing to do with him. He hadn't caused the arm to break. How could he? By saying words over an old souvenir? But what if it wasn't a souvenir? What if the stories about Father Baart were true?

By the time the school day was over, Johnny was a wreck. He was eaten up with guilt and fear and worry. What could he do? He couldn't tell Gramma or Grampa. They wouldn't understand. But he could tell the professor. The professor was a smart man and a wise man. When he had heard the whole story, he would know what to do.

Johnny was strangely silent during dinner that evening. Gramma and Grampa were used to his daydreaming during meals, but this was something different. He seemed to be worried, and his face was pale. Twice Grampa asked Johnny if anything was wrong, and twice Johnny said no, everything was fine. Finally, after dessert, Johnny cleared his throat and announced that he had a chess date with the professor this evening. This was a lie, of course. The professor didn't even know that he was coming.

"Don't stay out too late," said Gramma as Johnny got up to go. Gramma was a real bug about sleep. She was convinced that nine tenths of the things that were wrong with people were caused by lack of sleep.

"I won't," said Johnny.

"And please put on your sweater," Gramma added. "It's cold out there tonight. Remember, it's not summer yet."

"Uh-huh," said Johnny.

He walked out to the coat-tree in the front hall and took his sweater off the hook. As he put it on he found that strange images were floating around in his head. In his mind's eye he saw himself standing before the altar in the church, staring up at the gilded figures. Then he saw himself standing across the street from the church in the wintertime. Snow was blowing past, and somebody was standing on the steps of the church, waiting for him, but he couldn't tell who it was. Johnny shook his head. The images were gone. With a thoughtful look on his face he went to the door, opened it, and stepped outside.

It was a chilly April night. It had rained earlier, and the sidewalks glistened. Johnny walked across the porch and clumped down the steps. He stood for a moment, looking across at the professor's house. The lights were on in the study upstairs. But now that he was out here, Johnny realized that he did not have the faintest desire to go talk to his friend. He wanted to go someplace else instead. Suddenly he swung into motion. He trotted down the sidewalk, turned right, and kept on going.

A few minutes later Johnny was standing across the street from St. Michael's Church. He stared up at its massive dark shadow, and he realized that he was actually in the picture that he had seen in his mind a few minutes earlier. Only it wasn't wintertime, and there was no dark figure waiting for him on the steps. Still, Johnny couldn't shake the feeling that he had stepped into a dream. He felt strange, weirdly calm. Quickly he crossed the street. He mounted the steps and tugged at the iron ring. The door swung open, and he was inside, in the dimly lit vestibule. Johnny pushed the inner door open and stepped into the church.

At first he just stood there in the back, in the darkness under the choir loft. He drank in the musty, incensy, waxy smell. Two of the overhead lights were on. They cast a dim yellowish light in the cavernous interior of the church. Up in the sanctuary Johnny could see the gesturing, staring figures on the altarpiece. In its bracket on the sanctuary wall the red lamp flickered. Rows of empty pews stretched away before Johnny. Empty? Well, no . . . not quite. Somebody was sitting up in the front pew. Just sitting quietly and staring up at the altarpiece. The light was bad, but the person seemed to be a short, gray-haired man in a black overcoat. Johnny felt a sudden chill. He thought about the ghost of Father Baart. Then, in the next instant, Johnny realized that his imagination was running away with him again. He had been thinking all day about Eddie's broken arm and the figurine, and it had made him edgy. Lots of old people came to the church to pray, especially in the evening. It was nothing to get all worked up about.

Johnny slipped into a pew, knelt down, and made the sign of the cross. He stared up at the golden door of the tabernacle. Johnny wanted to get rid of his guilty feelings. He wanted to get rid of the feeling that he was the one who had broken Eddie's arm. He knew it was silly to think that a souvenir of Cairo, Illinois, was magic. But his guilt wouldn't go away. Now he wanted to say a prayer that would make him feel peaceful and happy again. Silently, his lips just barely moving, Johnny said the Act of Contrition:

> Oh my God, I am heartily sorry for having offended thee, and I detest all my sins because of thy just punishments. But most of all because I have offended thee, my God, who art all good and deserving of all my love. I firmly resolve, with the help of thy grace, to sin no more and to avoid the near occasion of sin. Amen.

After he had said this prayer, Johnny knelt, silent, his chin resting on his folded hands. He would have liked to hear the voice of God telling him that everything was okay. But all he heard was the rushing of blood in his ears and the swish of traffic passing outside. He felt better—a little better, anyway. And he decided, on the spur of the moment, that he would like to light a candle for his mother. He got up, sidled out of the pew, and walked down the aisle to the vigil-light rack near the confessional. He lit a candle and then knelt and said a brief prayer for his mother. He got up, and as he was turning around he got his first good look at the man who was sitting in the front pew. In a way it was a relief. This little man did not look in any way like the evil Father Baart. He had a bland freckled face and a little snub nose. His hair was iron-gray and was swept back in wings along the sides of his head. His eyebrows were black and arched, so that he had a permanently surprised look. The man was wearing a pin-striped gray suit, a gray vest, a black overcoat, and a gray tie with a pearl stickpin. His shoes were polished, and everything about him looked spotless and neat and prosperous.

As soon as the man saw that Johnny was looking at him, he smiled shyly.

"Good evening, young man," he said. "What brings you to the church so late at night, eh?"

Johnny moved closer. When he answered, he whispered. He always whispered in church. "I was saying a prayer for my mom," he said. "She died a little while ago."

"Ah!" said the man, and he nodded knowingly. "That is sad. I am sorry to hear it." Then, quite unexpectedly, he went on. "You know, young man," he said, fixing Johnny with his large surprised eyes, "I am a pretty good judge of character. And I think that you are a young man with a problem. Isn't that so?"

Johnny was startled. He didn't know what to say.

The man smiled. "Ah, it's true, isn't it? I can see it in your face." He patted the seat of the pew. "Would you care to sit down here and tell me all about it?"

To his own great surprise Johnny found himself sitting down next to the little man. And then he told him everything. It all came tumbling out, about Eddie's broken arm and the blue figurine and all. To Johnny, talking to the little man seemed as easy . . . well, as easy as walking across a room. The man was so warm and sympathetic. He shook his head and frowned when Johnny told him about the nasty things Eddie had done to him. And those large dark eyes seemed so wise, so knowing.

When Johnny had finished his tale, he sat silent, hands folded in his lap. He wondered what the man would say. At first the man said nothing. He stared thoughtfully at the floor. Then, at last, he spoke.

"Well, young fellow," said the man slowly, "it seems that you have a problem. Your problem is that you imagine things, and you worry too much. The figurine isn't magical—that much seems clear. But," he added oddly, "wouldn't it be fun to pretend that it was?"

Johnny was puzzled. "I don't get what you mean."

"Just this: you are afraid of this big bully Eddie. Maybe if you were to *pretend* to yourself that the blue figurine was magic, you would be able to stand up to him. It might give you . . . some unexpected strength. What do you think of that idea, eh?"

Johnny was still confused. "Would . . . would you explain that to me again, sir?"

The man smiled patiently. "What I'm suggesting is very simple. I'm merely saying that you should *pretend*. Use the powers of your imagination. Every morning before you go to school, rub the figurine and say some silly prayer. Make one up. Call upon the gods of Egypt if you want to—you'll find their names in any dictionary. You see, if you imagine that you're strong, you really *will* be strong! I think it'll help you—I really do."

Johnny frowned and bit his lip. He didn't like this plan—he didn't like it at all. "Look," he said slowly, "you . . . you have to understand. I wouldn't want to hurt anybody. I mean, what if the little blue statue really *is* magic? What if I used it to make somebody have an accident, or to kill them? I wouldn't—"

The little man burst into laughter. High-pitched, silvery laughter. "My, you *do* have an imagination!" he exclaimed, still laughing. "A real, grade-A imagination, that is for certain!" He laughed a bit more, and then suddenly he grew serious. He fixed Johnny with those uncanny large eyes. "Listen, young fellow," he said in a low, sincere voice, "I would not for the world have anything bad happen to you. Not for the *world*! I'm merely suggesting something that you can do to help yourself. People are funny creatures. If they think they're ugly, then they really are ugly. If they think they're weak, then they really are weak. Whatever you think you are, that's what you are. If you use that little blue figurine to convince yourself that you're strong, then maybe you really will become more confident, stronger. At least I think it's worth a try. Give it a try, and if you don't like the way this little game makes you feel, you can quit. How about it, eh? Will you try?"

As Johnny listened he found that he was agreeing with the man. The man's voice was low and purring and very persuasive. And his eyes . . . well, they were hypnotic. They were like great black pools. *Maybe it's a good idea*, thought Johnny. *Maybe it would work*.

"I . . . I guess I'd like to try it," said Johnny hesitantly.

The man smiled broadly. "Good!" he exclaimed enthusiastically. "Try it, and let me know if it works. I come in here often, just to sit and think or to pray. Stop in . . . oh, let's say in a week's time, and let me know how you're getting on. Good luck, by the way."

Johnny shook hands with the man and thanked him for listening to his problems. He started to get up, but the man reached out and laid his hand on his knee to stop him.

"Just a second," he said, smiling. "I have something for you." He reached into his vest pocket and took out a ring. "It's just a silly trinket, but it might help you with the little game that you're going to play. Here. Hold out your hand."

Johnny held out his hand, and the man laid the ring in it. Curious, Johnny looked down at what he was holding. It was a rather odd ring. It looked as if it was made from a bent nail. At the place where the two ends of the nail met, they held a small transparent stone that was tinted yellow. There was something under the stone. It looked like tiny slivers of wood, arranged to form the letter B.

"It's a monogram ring," said the man, tapping the stone with his forefinger. "My name is Beard. Robert Beard. The ring has been passed down through several generations of my family. It's worthless, except for its sentimental value. I thought you might like to have it."

Johnny gazed at the man wonderingly. He couldn't figure out why this total stranger was giving him an old family ring. But it felt good in his hand somehow. He liked it. "Thanks," he said, and he slipped it on to the third finger of his left hand. Johnny did not have a ring of his own at present. He had worn a silver Boy Scout ring for several years, but it had irritated the skin of his finger, and he had had to take it off. Now it felt good to have a ring again.

Johnny got up. Again he thanked the strange little man. Smiling blandly, the man waved good-bye and wished Johnny luck with the little game. Down the aisle Johnny walked, and through the two sets of doors. At the bottom of the stone steps he paused. There was a streetlamp nearby, and by its light he could see the ring. Way down in its depths the yellow stone was doing odd things. Johnny saw little flashes of iridescent blue and bloody red. He turned the ring back and forth and watched the way the light played over it. It was funny. He had come to the church feeling terribly guilty about Eddie's broken arm. Now he did not feel guilty at all. And he had made a new friend. Smiling in a satisfied way, Johnny walked away into the night.

CHAPTER SEVEN

❧❧

The next day after school Johnny went to the Public Library and consulted the unabridged dictionary. The unabridged was fun to use. It was a very thick and floppy book, and it stood on a swiveling wooden stand in a corner of the reference room. A lot of its definitions were strange and interesting, and the book was full of pictures of weird objects, like arbalests and brassards and undershot waterwheels. Johnny flipped straight to the *T*'s, because he had seen a picture of an Egyptian god there—at least he thought that he had. Ah. He was right. Here it was, a picture of the god Thoth. Thoth was a funny-looking thing. He had the body of a man and the head of an ibis, which is a hook-beaked bird that looks sort of like a heron. Thoth held in his hands a bunch of

Egyptian hieroglyphs. The dictionary said that Thoth was the god of magic and mathematics. He would be a good one to use in the game Johnny was going to play with the blue figurine. Johnny copied the name of Thoth down on a note pad he had brought with him. Then, idly, he flipped a couple of pages and found himself staring at the picture of another Egyptian god. This one was even more weird-looking. Her name was Touëris, and she had the body of a pregnant woman. Her head was the head of a hippopotamus. Touëris—according to the dictionary—was the goddess of childbirth, and of revenge. The revenge part was what interested Johnny. He copied Touëris's name down, closed the book, and went home.

That evening at dinner Grampa asked Johnny about his ring. He had noticed it the first time Johnny had showed up with it on, but he had not said anything then.

"That's really some ring, Johnny," said Grampa amiably as he sprinkled salt on his mashed potatoes. "Where'd you get it?"

Johnny's hand had been resting on the table. Now for some reason he jerked it away and hid it under the tablecloth. He felt shy about the ring. In school kids had noticed it, and at first they had made fun of it, claiming that it looked like a woman's engagement ring. To stop the kidding, Johnny had come up with a pretty snappy explanation. He had claimed that the ring was a Captain Midnight death ray ring. He said he had gotten it by sending in Ovaltine labels. But he did not think that an explanation like this would work on Grampa.

"I, uh, the professor . . . he gave it to me," said Johnny, glancing away evasively.

Grampa stared wonderingly at Johnny for a minute. He could not understand why Johnny was so nervous about the ring. Could Johnny have stolen it? No, Grampa told himself, that didn't seem very likely. Johnny was not the thieving kind. Grampa was curious, but he was not the sort of person who would give you the third degree. So he just dropped the subject and started talking about baseball.

That night Johnny dreamed a lot. At first he dreamed that he was a moth, fluttering about on a summer night. He kept hovering outside a lighted window, and through the window he could see Mr. Beard, the little man he had met in the church. The man was sitting at a table, reading. But no matter how much Johnny the moth beat at the window with his wings, the man never looked up. Then the dream shifted, and Johnny was outside R. Baart's antique store again. He went in as before, and there was the horrible old lady in the green eyeshade. But this time, instead of trying to drag him down into the grave behind the counter, she chased him around and around the shop, up steep rickety staircases, down long dark hallways lined with dusty bureaus and bookcases and looming dark bedsteads.

Johnny awoke around three in the morning, and he

felt exhausted. Exhausted, and strangely nervous. He got up, put on his slippers and bathrobe, and padded down the stairs. He tried the front door, but it was locked tight, as always. Then Johnny stood in the front hall listening. It was a still night. The apple tree outside the hall window hung perfectly motionless. But for some reason the house was making noise. All old houses make noises at night, creaks and cracks and pops. But this was different. It was a rustling noise, a strange ghostly whispering. As Johnny listened the noise died away, and the house was silent again. Eyes wide with wonder and fear, Johnny turned toward the stairs and slowly began to climb.

Johnny did not get much sleep that night. He kept waking up and glancing anxiously around, straining to hear strange sounds. The next morning he stood at his bureau in his rumpled pajamas. The face that stared back at him from the bureau mirror was red-eyed and woozy. On the clean white runner lay the ring Mr. Beard had given him. Johnny picked the ring up and turned it over in his hands. After the dreams he had had and the sounds he had heard in the night, he was beginning to wonder about the little game that Mr. Beard wanted him to play. Mr. Beard was a nice man—that was certainly true—and he was only trying to help Johnny. But what if the figurine really *was* magic? What if Eddie's broken arm hadn't been just a coincidence? Johnny fussed and fumed and thought some more, and as he thought he slipped the ring on his finger.

He looked at himself in the mirror and blinked. Things were suddenly clearer. How silly all his doubts and fears were! He ought to go ahead with the "magic" game. If he played the game, it would make him feel stronger and braver, and then he would *be* stronger and braver, just like Mr. Beard had said.

Johnny went to the closet and opened the door. He knelt down and took the blankets and magazines and sweat shirts off the black book. He opened the lid and took the figurine out. Holding it in his hands, he said the "prayer" that he had made up:

Thoth attend me! Touëris be my avenger! Let those who oppose me beware, for I will make them rue the day when they raised their hands against me! By the name of Amon-Ra I swear it!

Johnny paused. If he was expecting magical fireworks, he was disappointed. The blue figurine smiled up at him as always, but it looked and felt exactly the way it always had. No voices spoke to him out of the air. No thunder rolled. No dark clouds came rushing in to hide the morning sun.

Johnny felt slightly silly. He was glad there wasn't anyone in the room watching him. "This is a dumb idea," he muttered to himself. "It isn't gonna make me any braver or anything." He got up and started peeling off his pajama top. It would be time to go to school soon.

When Johnny walked into the church that morning, he suddenly remembered that it was the first day of May.

On the altar were fresh flowers, and the six tall candles were lit. May meant processions, with kids marching solemnly around the church, and hymns and incense and organ music. That was all right with Johnny. He loved parades and processions. Later, after Mass, Johnny was up in the seventh-grade classroom, sitting at his desk. Sister Electa had not called the class to order yet. In fact she was not even in the room. So everybody was just talking and goofing off. With his finger Johnny idly drew circles in the layer of polish on the top of his desk. For no reason at all his prayer book popped into his head. Johnny was very proud of his prayer book. His dad had given it to him as a going-away present, before he had sent Johnny off to live with Gramma and Grampa in Duston Heights. Johnny used the prayer book every day. It had a black cover of genuine leather, with a gold cross stamped on the spine. The pages were made of onionskin paper, thin and whispery, and the top edge of each page was gilded, so when the book was closed, a glimmering gold bar shone out at you. There were illustrations all through the book, and fancy capital letters, and there were two bookmark ribbons, one purple, the other red. The prayer book was one of Johnny's prized possessions. It felt good just to hold the book in his hand.

Smiling he reached down to the briefcase that stood on the floor next to his desk. The prayer book was in there with his other books. But Johnny's smile faded when he saw that the clasp on his briefcase was undone.

Johnny was very fussy about the clasp. He always did it up after he had taken something out of the briefcase. So it seemed pretty likely that somebody had been fooling around with his stuff. Alarmed, Johnny reached down and lifted the briefcase up into his lap. He opened the flap and peered inside. He could hardly believe it. His prayer book was gone!

Angry tears sprang to Johnny's eyes. Who could have done such a dirty, rotten thing? His mind began to race. Had the briefcase been out of his sight this morning? Johnny thought hard. He had had it with him in the pew this morning, and then he had brought it over to the school, and since then he had been sitting here at his desk, except for one brief trip to the pencil sharpener. So who . . .

And then it came to him. Phil. Phil Absen, the kid behind him.

Phil Absen was a weird kid. There was something wrong with his head, and so he did strange things and said strange things. Gramma had often said (grumblingly) that Phil was proof of the fact that Catholic schools would take *anybody*. Johnny didn't like Phil much, but he didn't dislike him much either. And up until now he hadn't figured that Phil was a thief.

Johnny turned and looked at Phil. He was pretending to be very busy, leafing madly through his geometry book. When Phil saw Johnny giving him the fisheye, he got even busier. It seemed pretty plain to Johnny that Phil was the guilty one. Who else could it be?

Johnny felt his face getting flushed. Anger was building up inside him. He wanted to grab Phil by the collar and shake the truth out of him.

"Hey, Phil!" he began loudly. "Did you—"

But then Sister Electa's voice cut in. She was summoning them all to attention. She was asking them all to stand and recite the Pledge of Allegiance. Johnny bit his lip. He turned and got up. He would settle with Phil later.

All through the first two morning classes Johnny steamed about his missing prayer book. He kept hoping that Sister Electa would leave the room so he could turn around and give Phil holy hell. Johnny was scared of kids like Eddie Tompke, but he was not scared of Phil. Phil was a real wimp, and even Johnny could terrorize him if he set his mind to it. And if Sister Electa ever left the room, Johnny *would* terrorize him. He would turn around and grab Phil's arm and squeeze it and make him give the prayer book back. It would be as simple as that— at least Johnny hoped it would be.

But the first two class periods passed, and Sister Electa never left the room. Then eleven o'clock came. It was time for religion class—but Sister had a surprise for everyone. Instead of holding the regular class, she announced, they and all the other students were going to go over to the church and start rehearsing for the May procession. Some kids groaned, and Sister Electa glared sternly at them. Then she walked quickly to her desk and dinged the little hand bell. Everybody stood up, and then, beginning with the row nearest the door, they began to file out of the room, just the way they did during a fire drill.

A little later Johnny was with the other kids, marching slowly around, two by two, inside the vast, dark, echoing church. Nuns were rushing here and there, making sure that the lines were straight and bawling out kids who were fooling around. Mrs. Hoxter was playing the electric organ up in the choir loft, and the kids were singing:

> Bring flowers of the fairest
> Bring flowers of the rarest
> From garden and woodland and hillside and vale . . .

As Johnny shuffled moodily along he began to wonder why he had thought that processions were fun. This one was about as interesting as watching grass grow. Of course it was only a rehearsal. They hadn't even chosen the girl who would crown the Blessed Virgin's statue yet. Johnny wondered who they would choose. Probably Mary Jo Potter. The sisters were the ones who got to choose the girl, and Mary Jo was so holy and pious and religious and sweet that it was sickening. . . .

The procession came to a sudden, lurching, bumping stop. Something had gone wrong up in front, though Johnny couldn't tell what. Now that the marching had stopped, he turned and began looking around in a vague, aimless way. Suddenly he stopped. He had seen something that made him boiling mad. Halfway back along the line stood Phil Absen. And he was holding Johnny's prayer book in his hands.

Johnny had trouble controlling himself. He was a pretty mild-mannered kid most of the time, but when he lost his temper, he lost it. He knew that Phil was a little weak in the head, but all the same, this was too much. Just a little teeny bit *too much*! Johnny clenched his fists and gritted his teeth. He wanted to jump out of line and tear back there and snatch the book out of Phil's hands. But, as angry as he was, he knew better than to do that. Sister Electa—or some other nun—would climb all over him if he started a fight in the church. So Johnny controlled his anger. There would be time to settle with good old Phil later.

The rehearsal for the May procession only lasted an hour, but to Johnny it seemed like it went on forever. Finally, though, around noon the nuns decided to call it quits. Streams of talking and laughing kids poured out through the three doors in the front of the church. Johnny went running out with the rest. He paused on the sidewalk, and he squinted and winced. After an hour in the dusky gloom of the church the light made his nearsighted eyes hurt. But when the pain passed, Johnny found that—once again—he was staring at Phil Absen. There he was, out by the bicycle rack, with the prayer book under his arm. He had a very pious, prissy look on his face, and he was talking to Sister Electa. Well, this was just too much. Johnny took off on the run, and he didn't stop till he came to where the two of them were standing.

"Hey, Sister!" Johnny exclaimed breathlessly. "Phil stole my prayer book! That's my prayer book! Make him give it back!"

Phil stared at Johnny with wide, scared eyes. He clutched the prayer book to his chest. "It's *not* his, Sister! He's lyin'! This's *my* prayer book. My . . . my mom gave it to me."

"I'm not a liar, but *he* is!" Johnny yelled, pointing a trembling finger at Phil. "He's a dirty, rotten liar! Sister, make him give it back! It's mine, I swear to God it is!"

The kids who had been standing and talking outside the church now crowded around Phil and Johnny. They knew that something was up. Somebody was going to get in trouble, and they wanted to watch.

Sister Electa looked from Johnny to Phil and back to Johnny again. She seemed perplexed, but she was determined to stay in control of the situation. "John," she said with a pained look on her face, "I know you're upset, but please try to lower your voice. And it is not a good idea, at any time, to use God's name in a loose way. Now then!" Sister Electa folded her arms under the scapular of her gown. She turned to Phil. "Phillip," she said in a mild but firm voice, "John here has accused you of taking his prayer book. I know John, and I know that he doesn't usually run around making wild accusations. However, it is possible that he has made a mistake in this case. Now, are you *sure* that that prayer book is yours?"

Phil's eyes grew wider and gogglier. It was clear that he was scared out of his mind. Still, though, he clung to the book. "It is *too* mine!" he said in a loud, childish voice. "He's a liar, Sister! He's a real liar!"

Sister Electa stared pityingly at Phil. She knew him pretty well, and she knew he had problems. She was well aware that there was something wrong with Phil's mind. Most of the time she tried to treat him just like any other twelve-year-old. But right now he was acting like a kid of six, and she felt she had to handle him differently.

Sister Electa unfolded her arms. She held out a well-washed hand. "Phillip," she said gently, "could I see the prayer book?"

Reluctantly Phil offered her the prayer book. Sister Electa took it, and then she turned to Johnny. "Now, John!" she said in a brisk, businesslike way. "Are there any identifying marks in this book? Is your name written in it anywhere?"

"It sure is, Sister. My dad wrote my name on the blank page in the front. Look and see if it's there."

Sister Electa opened the book. The flyleaf was gone. It had been torn out, torn out roughly. A ragged strip of white paper still protruded from the binding.

Sister Electa was silent for a moment. Then she looked searchingly, accusingly at Phil and once again held out her hand.

"Phillip," she said in a commanding voice, "I'd like to see *everything* that's in your pockets!"

Several of the kids in the crowd snickered and laughed.

Phil went white, but he did as he was told. First he pulled out a very dirty handkerchief and gave it to the nun. The crowd roared, but Sister Electa remained stern and unamused.

"Very good, Phillip. Now the other pocket, if you please."

Phil dug his hand into the other pocket and gave Sister Electa a handful of change. Still, however, she was not satisfied.

"Turn both your pockets all the way out," she said.

Phil did this, and a small wad of paper dropped from his left-hand pants pocket. The nun stooped and picked it up. Without a word she handed it to Johnny. With difficulty he uncrumpled the tight little wad of paper. But even before he had done this, he knew what he had: It was the missing flyleaf.

Suddenly Phil Absen started to cry. His childish face got all red and twisted up. He raised a trembling finger and pointed into the crowd. "Eddie Tompke made me do it!" he wailed. "It's his fault! He told me to do it!"

Johnny whirled and looked where Phil was pointing. Sure enough, there on the edge of the crowd stood Eddie, broken arm and all. There was a cynical, crooked grin on his face.

Sister Electa glowered skeptically at Phil. "Young man," she said severely, "don't try to blame things on other people when they're your own fault! Now, I'm going to give this prayer book back to John Dixon, and I'm also going to ask you to tell him that you're sorry you took it. And I'm afraid that you're going to have to stay after school today and have a little talk with me. Stealing is a somewhat more serious matter than you seem to think it is. Now, tell John that you're sorry you took his prayer book."

Still sniffling, Phil turned to Johnny. He stared at Johnny's shoes and blew his nose before he spoke. "I'm sorry I took it," he said in a dull, defeated monotone, "but like I said, Eddie—"

"*Please!*" exclaimed Sister Electa, cutting Phil off. "Please stop trying to blame others for what you did! Now, Phillip, go into the school and wash your face and pull yourself together. As for the rest of you," she added, turning to the crowd of kids who were still eagerly watching, "please find something else to do with your time. Go eat your lunches. You've only got half an hour till classes begin again. Go on, all of you! Make yourselves scarce!" Sister Electa made shooing motions with her hands.

The crowd broke up. Johnny thanked Sister Electa hurriedly and turned away. He should have felt triumphant, but he didn't. Something was bothering him. Phil had said that Eddie made him steal the prayer book. Sister Electa did not believe Phil, but Johnny did. Eddie liked to boss around weak, helpless kids, and Phil was about as weak and helpless as they come. Even with a broken arm Eddie could be pretty terrifying. He had probably threatened to do all sorts of nasty things to Phil unless he followed orders.

As Johnny was still standing there, thinking, he suddenly felt somebody's hand patting him on the back. He turned. It was Eddie.

"Boy, old Absen-minded can really tell 'em, can't he?" Eddie chortled. "Glad you got your prayer book back. They oughta toss that kid in the booby hatch! What a liar!"

Still chortling, Eddie walked away. Johnny watched him go. That settled it. Eddie would never have done what he had just done unless he was the guilty one. Johnny felt angry, but he also felt helpless and depressed. How long was he going to have to put up with Eddie? Would Eddie follow him around all through eighth grade, playing dirty tricks on him and making his life miserable?

Johnny did not have any answers to these questions. So he went back to the school building, clumped down the stairs to the basement lunchroom, and ate the sandwich and banana that he had brought with him. The rest of the school day passed in its usual way. Social studies and arithmetic for the last two hours of the day, the final prayer and the ringing of the bell for dismissal. And then all the kids swarmed down the worn, creaky stairs and out the front door into the sunlight. As usual Johnny was one of the last to leave. And when he finally did walk out the door, briefcase in hand, he didn't feel like going home. Not right away, anyway. So he decided to go down and walk by the river.

The Merrimack River, one of the widest and longest

rivers in New England, flowed through the middle of Duston Heights. Along its banks stood abandoned factories, long red brick buildings with tall brick smokestacks rising above them. Many years ago these factories had made cloth, but now they were closed, and their narrow windows were broken. Johnny liked the old factories. They were almost like haunted houses. As he walked along the grass-grown sidewalks of Water Street he peered up at the buildings that towered over him. High up, set in the brick walls, were little red terra-cotta decorations, leering monster faces or the solemn bearded masks of—Johnny imagined—Greek gods. Or you might see a stone plaque that said LEVERETT BROTHERS EST 1882. And here and there in the empty spaces between the buildings you might see an old rusted piece of machinery or a wooden clock face that had once been in a cupola somewhere.

After he had walked for two or three blocks, Johnny came to a place where a weedy courtyard opened out between two buildings. At the far end of the courtyard was a low half-ruined brick wall. Set neatly in a row on top of the wall were some old glass bottles. And standing there, slinging rocks at the bottles with his good arm, was Eddie Tompke.

Johnny froze. For a moment he just stood there watching. Eddie hadn't seen him yet. He was busy slinging away, throwing sidearm and then overhand, imitating the motions of a big-league baseball pitcher. His aim was pretty good. Pieces of broken glass lay at the base of the wall. Johnny wondered what he ought to do. Should he just slink on past, go about his business? Normally that was what he would have done. But Johnny was feeling strange. A force was rising up inside him, something irresistible. It was this force that made him do what he did next.

"Hey, Eddie!" he yelled suddenly. "You made Phil steal my prayer book, didn't you? You rotten flatheaded creep, I hope you fall down a manhole and break your other arm! You hear what I said, you rotten creep? You hear me?" Johnny gasped and turned pale. He hadn't meant to yell like that. It had all just come pouring out of him, almost as if somebody else was using his body and his vocal chords. Now what was going to happen?

Eddie turned around slowly. His mouth was set in a tense scowl, and his eyes were like two gray stones. When he spoke, his voice was dangerously calm.

"Come over here and say that, John baby."

Johnny was terrified. He wanted to run, but his feet wouldn't move. Even with a broken arm Eddie could make mincemeat out of him. The muscles in both his arms were like ropes, and his chest was like a cement wall. He would break his glasses and give him two black eyes and a split lip. He would beat Johnny to a pulp.

"I . . . I . . ." Johnny began, but he couldn't get the words out. Rooted to the spot with fear, he watched as Eddie began walking slowly toward him. And then something strange and totally unexpected happened. Johnny felt a sharp pain in his ring finger, and it seemed to him that the yellow stone flashed. And then a strong wind began to blow. It sprang up out of nowhere and blew past Johnny. The bushes that grew in the courtyard flailed madly to and fro. Bits of paper sailed up into the air, and a cloud of yellowish dust flew at Eddie. Coughing and sputtering, Eddie staggered backward. The wind blew harder and threw him, stumbling and reeling, against the brick wall. Bottles flew this way and that, and when Eddie stuck out a hand to steady himself, it came down on a piece of broken glass.

Eddie howled and jerked his hand toward his mouth. He sucked at the bleeding cut. Then silence fell. The wind died as suddenly as it had sprung up, and the yellow dust settled. Eddie looked at Johnny, and Johnny looked at Eddie. And which of them was more frightened it would have been hard to say.

CHAPTER EIGHT

It was a bright, sunshiny Saturday in May, and the professor was up on the square Italian cupola that jutted above the roof of his house. He was wearing overalls, his mouth was full of nails, and he had a hammer in his hand. The cupola had windows all around and a tiled roof with a silly wooden finial sprouting from it. All around the cupola rickety scaffolding had been built, and attached to the cupola roof was a fantastic framework of wooden slats, braces, joists, and whatnot. Someday, when it was finished, this framework would support an elaborate radio aerial. The professor was a wild Red Sox fan. He loved to listen to the Sox on the radio while he corrected his students' papers. The problem was this: WITS in Boston was the only station that carried the baseball games, and its signal was pretty faint by the time it reached Duston Heights. But the professor was confident that his superduper whizbang aerial would solve the problem. He had been reading up on aerials in *Mechanix Illustrated* and other handyman magazines, and in his study was a blueprint that he had drawn up, all by himself. Now if he could only get the job done, everything would be fine.

But as he worked the professor frowned and muttered to himself. He was worried. Not about his work but about Johnny. It was May 10, ten days after Johnny's run-in with Eddie Tompke. And in all that time the professor had not seen Johnny to talk with, not once. Normally Johnny came over three or four times a week for chess and conversation and chocolate cake. But not now. At first the professor had felt hurt. Then he had told himself that he was an old fool, that Johnny had—no doubt—found some young friend who was fun to be with. But then he began to watch for Johnny out of the front windows of his house. And what he saw alarmed him. Johnny was never with anyone. He always walked alone, head down, briefcase in hand. And he looked awful. His face was very pale, and there were dark circles under his eyes. He looked as if he had not slept for a week.

And so the professor was concerned. He wanted to know what was wrong. So far he had resisted the urge to butt in on the Dixons' family affairs. He couldn't imagine that Gramma and Grampa were mistreating

Johnny. That did not seem possible. But then, what *was* going on?

The professor drove in another nail. The framework creaked and shuddered, and the professor growled at it. He ordered it to hold together. From somewhere below a door slammed. The professor glanced over and saw Johnny plodding down the front steps of his house. Now he was moving along the sidewalk, head forward, hands folded behind his back. *Oh, this is just unbearable!* grumped the professor to himself. *I have got to go see the Dixons, or I will go out of my ever-loving mind!* And slowly he began to clamber down the scaffold.

A few minutes later the professor was knocking at the front door of the Dixon home. Presently the door rattled open. There stood Grampa. He was wearing a blue denim apron, and his sleeves were rolled up. In one hand he held a hypodermic syringe. The professor was not surprised at this. He knew that Gramma Dixon had diabetes and that Grampa had to give her an insulin shot once every day. Normally in this kind of situation the professor would have made some sort of wisecrack. He would have called Grampa Young Dr. Malone or some such thing. But he was not in a wisecracking mood. And he could see from Grampa's long face that he was not feeling very jokey either.

"Hi, Henry," said the professor, smiling faintly. "All right if I come in?"

"Sure. Come on out to the kitchen. It's shot time, as you can see. It'll be over in a minute."

The professor followed Grampa out to the kitchen. There he found Gramma, sitting at the white enameled table. The sleeve of her dress was rolled up, and on the table was a bottle of rubbing alcohol. Nearby lay some wads of cotton. The professor sat down, and he politely turned away his face as Grampa shoved the needle into Gramma's arm. Then, when it was over and Grampa was rinsing the hypodermic in the sink, the professor cleared his throat harrumphily.

"I came over to talk to you two about Johnny," he began. "I . . . well, I'm a bit worried about him."

"So 're we," said Gramma, frowning. "He don't sleep good at night, an' he has bad dreams. Woke up screamin' an' yellin' to beat the band the other night. Scared the dickens outa me, but he wouldn't tell us what the heck was wrong."

"He don't eat good, either," added Grampa as he dried the glass hypodermic tube with a linen towel. "Just picks at his food like a little bird. I asked him the other day if somethin' was wrong, but he said no, everything was fine. Can you beat that? I don't know what to make of it. Do *you* know what's eatin' him, Rod? I mean, you're his friend an' all, so I thought maybe . . ."

"Well, you thought wrong," said the professor gloomily. "I haven't seen him to talk to in about two weeks. I came over here hoping that you two might enlighten me." The professor gazed disconsolately around the room. He looked at the hexagonal red electric clock that hung over the stove and at the rack of test tubes that stood on the windowsill. "I saw him going somewhere the other night. Do you know where he goes?"

Grampa shrugged. "Far as I know, he goes down to the church. He says he wants to light a candle for his mom an' pray. I don't see anything wrong with that, do you?"

The professor shook his head. "No. Not if that's what he's really doing. But you know—with your permission —I think I'm going to follow him one of these nights to see where he goes. I'm good at tailing people. I was an intelligence officer during World War I. My code name was the Crab."

Gramma laughed loudly, and the professor glared at her. "What's so funny about that?" he snapped. "I don't see anything to laugh at, do you, Henry?"

Grampa bit his lip and shook his head solemnly. And then, to cover up the giggling fit that had come over him, he rushed over to the stove and poured the professor a nice hot cup of coffee. Gramma, Grampa, and the professor talked for a while longer, and they cooked up a scheme: Grampa would call up the professor the next time he knew that Johnny was going on one of his nighttime visits to the church. Then the professor would shadow Johnny, and . . . well, they all three hoped that this would help them get to the bottom of the mystery. They cared for Johnny a lot, and they did not want anything bad to happen to him.

As it turned out, the three conspirators got a chance

to put their plan into action sooner than they might have expected. That evening at dinner Johnny announced that he was going down to the church to pray. When? Oh, around eight o'clock. Gramma looked at Grampa, and Grampa stared at the saltcellar. Both of them tried hard to act unconcerned.

Gramma smiled weakly and said in a falsely cheerful voice, "Well, that's fine! I sure think it's good when a boy your age goes to church without bein' dragged there by the heels." Then she looked hard at Johnny and added in a more serious tone, "Johnny?"

Johnny laid down his fork and stared back at Gramma. He felt defensive. His guard was up. What did she want to know? "Yeah, Gramma? What is it?"

The tone of Johnny's voice was so unfriendly that Gramma was startled. She glanced quickly down and began to toy with a piece of celery on her plate. "Well . . . your grampa and me were wonderin' if . . . if you felt okay these days. I mean, if there's anythin' on your mind, we could . . . well, kinda help you with it."

Johnny's eyes were stony. "I don't know what you're talkin' about, Gramma. I'm all right. I just wanta go down to the church to pray tonight, that's all. Is that okay with you?"

Gramma nodded helplessly. And that was the end of the conversation. The meal went on in silence. After dessert Johnny went upstairs to his room, closed the door, and bolted it. He sat down on his bed and stared around at the old-fashioned furniture. The tall gloomy clothespress with the scrolled decorations on the front. The marble-topped bureau with the mirror. The bristly brown armchair, the old pictures in heavy black frames, and the Motorola radio on the scarred black end table by the window.

And then the hard, tense look on Johnny's face melted. He burst into tears.

Ever since the first of May, Johnny had been living inside a nightmare. He was hearing and seeing strange things, and he was doing things without knowing why he did them. He felt that he was in danger—terrible danger—but he was scared to death to tell anybody about it.

First there was the figurine. It was magic, it was enchanted—he knew that now. Every morning, as regular as clockwork, Johnny would get out of bed, take the figurine from its hiding place, stroke it, and say the prayer to Thoth and Touëris. He had to—he wasn't sure why he did this, but he knew he had to. And at night sometimes, as he was lying in bed trying to sleep, Johnny would hear whispering coming from the closet where the figurine was hidden. Sometimes he almost thought he could figure out what the whispering voice was saying. And there was the ring. It was magic too. It was connected with the figurine in some way that Johnny didn't understand. He wanted to take the ring off, but he was scared to. It hurt his finger sometimes, made the bone of his finger ache and throb, so that he wanted to cry out with the pain. But something in his mind, an insistent voice, told him that he couldn't take the ring off, not even for a minute. If he did, awful things would happen to him.

And then there were the dreams. Over and over, every night, Johnny had the dream about R. Baart's antique shop. Over and over the old lady in the green eyeshade chased him through endless rooms, up endless cobwebbed staircases, or dragged him down into dark, earth-smelling, wormy graves. And he would wake up many times during the night, and he would look around wildly, convinced that there was somebody in his room. But when he turned on the lights, there was never anyone there.

Johnny blew his nose and wiped his eyes. He smiled wanly. One good thing had been accomplished: Eddie Tompke was scared to death of him. After that afternoon down by the factories Eddie had avoided Johnny like the plague. Whenever he passed Eddie on the stairs or in the lunchroom or wherever, Eddie would give him this goggle-eyed, frightened stare and hurry past. Johnny had always daydreamed about having power, the power to scare off bullies. But now that he had the power, he didn't want it—not if it was going to make him feel like this. Johnny was miserable, utterly miserable. He wanted to tell Gramma and Grampa that he was frightened, but something—the ring, or some other awful and evil force —forced him to keep his mouth shut. Johnny felt like somebody inside a glass-walled soundproof prison. He pounded on the walls, but nobody heard. He screamed, but no sound came out.

Nervously Johnny glanced at the Big Ben alarm clock that ticked loudly on his bureau. It was a quarter to eight. He'd better get a move on. He didn't want to stay out too late. And where was he going? He was going to St. Michael's Church, to see if he could find Mr. Beard, the little man who had given him the ring. Mr. Beard had said he would see Johnny in about a week's time. But had he meant a week exactly, or what? Johnny didn't know, but he did know one thing: He desperately needed to talk to the man. Night after night he had gone down to the church hoping that Mr. Beard would show up. But he was never there. Did Mr. Beard know that the ring was magic? That was another large question in Johnny's mind. If he did know, that meant that he was evil, that he had conned Johnny into taking the ring. For his own peace of mind Johnny wanted to think that Mr. Beard was a nice guy, that he hadn't known anything about the awful powers that lay hidden in the ring. Somewhere Johnny had read a story about a magic amulet that hadn't seemed magic until somebody said a secret prayer over it. Maybe this was what had happened. Maybe the ring had passed down through Mr. Beard's family for generations, and nobody had known that it was enchanted. And then Johnny had aroused the sleeping magic with his prayer to Thoth and Touëris. And what about the figurine? That was another deep, dark, frightening mystery that

Johnny couldn't fathom. But he felt that he could deal with the blue figurine if he could ever get the ring off his finger. He was hoping, hoping frantically, that Mr. Beard would turn out to be an okay guy, that he would be willing to help. If he knew something about the ring, something that would allow Johnny to get rid of it, then, later, he would take a hammer and smash the smiling blue idol into a million million tiny blue pieces.

Johnny got up and glanced nervously around the room. He stared at the closet door, and for a second he had the horrible unreasoning fear that the door would open and the blue figurine would come waddling out, like a windup toy soldier. Johnny shuddered and left the room, turning out the light as he went.

Outside, in front of the house, Johnny paused. It was a chilly May evening. He was glad he had his suede jacket on. He glanced up and down the street. Lights were on in most of the houses, but the professor's house was a dark mass of shadow. He was probably out at the movies or visiting one of his friends. Johnny felt alone and frightened. He listened to the wind that was rustling the new May leaves on the trees. Suddenly he had a great urge to rush across the street into the professor's house and turn on the living room lights and sit there until the professor came home. Johnny could do this if he wanted to. The professor had given him a door key—it was on the key ring in the pocket of his jacket. Johnny pondered. Then he felt a sharp twinge of pain in his ring finger, and that made up his mind for him. The professor couldn't help him with the ring. He had to find Mr. Beard. Johnny clenched his teeth. He turned suddenly to the right, like a soldier making a turn on a drill field. Swinging his arms, he began to march down Fillmore Street.

The sound of Johnny's footsteps grew fainter and then died away. He had disappeared into the darkness at the end of the street. Now, out of the shadows that shrouded the professor's house, a figure stepped. It was Professor Childermass himself. He was wearing his ratty tweed coat and a wide-brimmed felt fedora. On his feet were tennis shoes. With quick, springy, soundless steps he began to move down the sidewalk, and soon he too had disappeared.

When Johnny got to the church, he was—once again —disappointed. There was nobody there but Mrs. McGinnis. Mrs. McGinnis was a tall, big-boned, and rather silly old lady who wore floppy wide-brimmed hats and held her head to one side, as if she lived in an attic room with a sloping ceiling. She was kneeling in the front pew and thumbing her rosary beads. Johnny was more than disappointed—he felt almost desperate. What had happened to Mr. Beard? Why didn't he come here anymore? But as Johnny was turning away to go something caught his eye. Something small and white lying on the seat of the last pew. It was a piece of note-paper with writing on it. Probably it was somebody's grocery list. Why was he wasting time gaping at it? But it was oddly fascinating all the same. Johnny bent over and picked the note up. He saw spindly, scrawly handwriting. The note said:

Meet me in Duston Park.
Yours very truly,
Robt. Beard

Johnny was startled and a bit amused. What an odd duck Mr. Beard was! And why had he left the note here in the back pew, in the darkness? How could he be so sure that Johnny would find it? Nevertheless, he *had* found it. And he knew where Duston Park was. It was over on the other side of the river, about a fifteen minute walk from the church. Should he go? Johnny felt that he had to. He set his mouth in a determined frown. Abruptly he turned and walked out of the church. The swinging doors queaked and quacked behind him as he went.

Duston Park was over in Cranbrook, which was the snooty part of Duston Heights. The park was a long grassy triangle with a rail fence around it. It was surrounded by houses and one tall white colonial church. Inside the park were benches and a few young maple trees, and in the center of the park was a bronze statue of Hannah Duston. She stood there, tense and defiant, on her high granite pedestal. In one hand she held a tomahawk, and in the other, ten Indian scalps. Hannah was a famous woman. She had scalped ten Indians long ago on an island in the Merrimack River, to get even with them for having murdered her baby right before her eyes. On the base of the statue was a list of the people who had paid for the statue and an inscription in Latin. But her name was not on the statue, and unless you knew the story of Hannah Duston, you might have wondered who the lady with the hatchet was and what she had done.

When Johnny got to the park, it was deserted. There was an old-fashioned streetlamp in the middle of the park, and a bench under it, but there was no one sitting on the bench. Once again Johnny's heart sank. He had walked as fast as he could. Now what was he going to do? With a dejected sigh he slumped on into the park and sat down on the bench by the lamp. He glanced at his watch. It was getting on toward nine. He didn't dare stay too long—Gramma would be worried about him. He decided that he would wait for exactly ten minutes and then get up and leave.

Minutes passed. Johnny hummed to himself and looked aimlessly this way and that. He looked at the greenish bronze statue that held a tomahawk poised over his head. He peered across the street at the Unitarian church, with its six white Corinthian pillars and its tall graceful colonial spire. Now as he watched he saw somebody step out of the darkness next to the church. The figure moved forward quickly into the light. It was Mr. Beard. Pausing briefly at the curb, he started to cross the street. Mr. Beard was wearing his black coat and a kind of black hat called a homburg. When he saw Johnny, he glanced impatiently at him. Mr. Beard did not seem to be in a good mood.

"Well," he said snappishly as he sat down on the bench, "you certainly took your time about getting here." He glared at Johnny, and his large black eyes seemed mean and hard.

Johnny was utterly confused by this remark. What was Mr. Beard talking about? He sounded as if he and Johnny had made a date to meet at some certain time. Johnny felt hurt, and there was also something in Mr. Beard's manner that frightened him. He wanted to get up and leave. But Mr. Beard's great dark eyes fascinated him. He stayed where he was.

Mr. Beard smiled, but it was a crooked, lopsided smile. "And what is on your mind, pray tell?"

Johnny held out his hand. "The . . . the ring . . ." he stammered. "It . . . it's . . ."

"Magical?" said Mr. Beard in a cold, mocking voice. "Magical? Of course it is. Does that bother you? Eh? Eh?"

Johnny was stunned. So Mr. Beard had known all along that the ring was magic! A vague, shapeless fear began to form in Johnny's mind. What else did Mr. Beard know? And why, why on earth, had he given him this ring?

Mr. Beard took off his hat and laid it on the bench. His well-combed grayish-white hair seemed to glimmer and sparkle in the lamplight. It made Johnny think of snow.

And now Johnny noticed something else. Although he looked neat and well cared for, there was a faint musty odor about Mr. Beard. As if, perhaps, his overcoat had been kept in a damp, dark closet too long. Again Johnny had an overwhelming urge to jump up and run for home. But Mr. Beard's enormous eyes held him riveted to his seat.

"So the ring bothers you. Well, that's too bad," crooned Mr. Beard. His smile was cold and pitiless. "Yes, that is very, very sad. Perhaps this will help."

Mr. Beard raised his left hand. And suddenly Johnny felt as if his whole left arm was on fire. Pain shot up toward his shoulder, and the ring pinched, pinched horribly, far more painfully than Eddie's scissors had pinched. It felt as if red-hot pincers were squeezing his finger to the bone. Johnny's breath was taken away by the suddenness of this attack. He writhed to and fro and gasped, "*Stop! Stop! Please stop!*"

Mr. Beard lowered his hand, and the pain stopped.

"There now," he said, grinning evilly, "isn't that better? Of course it is. But I'm afraid you can't take the ring off. That is not part of my little plan. This should teach you to be careful about accepting gifts from strangers. You can never tell what the gift may turn out to be. But you accepted my ring, my little friend, and you will have to accept the consequences."

Mr. Beard chuckled. It was a low, weird chuckle that raised the hairs on the back of Johnny's neck. Johnny's face was pale and haggard. Sweat was streaming down his cheeks and stood in beads on his forehead. He felt like some small frightened animal caught in a trap.

Mr. Beard went on grinning. It was a goblinish grin, a grin that seemed to change the features of his face. "Haven't you guessed yet who I am?" he asked suddenly. *"Haven't you guessed?"*

Mr. Beard's voice sounded strange and wavery now. It was like the sound you get when a radio is not tuned in quite right. *Haven't you guessed? Haven't you guessed?* The question seemed to echo endlessly in Johnny's brain. And now the air around him was shimmering, wavering like water. And Mr. Beard's face changed, changed slowly, to the face of an old man with an overhanging forehead, a jutting chin, a hawkish nose, and deep-set, burning eyes. Instead of an overcoat he wore a heavy black woolen cape, and around his neck was a stiff white collar, the collar of a Catholic priest.

Johnny stared. He felt as if his eyes were going to pop out of their sockets. His forehead throbbed, and he was afraid that he might faint. Meanwhile across the street a shadowy figure was watching. It was the professor. He was crouched behind a large evergreen bush in somebody's front yard. What he saw was Johnny sitting on a bench that was bathed in the pale light of the street lamp. Johnny was staring hard at something, but the professor could not figure out what that something was. As far as he could tell, the bench—except for Johnny—was empty and bare.

CHAPTER NINE

The Sessions clock on the Dixons' sideboard was striking
ten as Johnny opened the front door and stumbled in.
Johnny felt numb and unbelievably tired. Every bone in
his body ached. He felt as if he had stayed up three
nights in a row without sleep. Was he awake or asleep
now? It was hard to tell. He had seen the ghost of Father
Baart. And the ghost had given him orders that in seven
days he must return to Duston Park. He had to return
at midnight next Friday, and he had to bring the blue
figurine with him. He did not know why he had to do
this, but he had been given very strict orders. He had to
do this or he would die. The ring could kill him—this
he had been told. He had also been told that the ring
would be taken from him that night. He would be set

free then, and nothing bad would happen to him. His life would be his own to live. But if he told anyone about the midnight meeting, or if he failed to show up, then he would die—he would die in horrible torment.

Dully, mechanically, Johnny unzipped his suede jacket and hung it on the coat-tree. He gazed blearily around at the friendly hall furniture. At the china umbrella stand, and the old pictures, and the deer head that was missing a glass eye. These things failed to comfort him. Was Grampa still up? The door of the living room was open, and a narrow bar of light shone out into the dark hall. Johnny heard a chair creak, and then he heard Grampa's voice.

"Johnny? That you?"

"Yeah, Grampa," Johnny answered wearily. He shuffled to the open doorway and stopped. "I'm sorry I was out so late."

Grampa shrugged. "It's okay. Your gramma's the worrier in this family, but she's gone to bed. I'm headed that way too, the way I feel." Grampa paused and looked at Johnny in a guarded way. "Do a lot o' prayin', did you?"

"Uh-huh. Well, g'night, Grampa."

"G'night, Johnny. Sleep tight."

Johnny stood in the doorway a moment longer, staring in at Grampa. He had an overwhelming urge to rush in and fall down on his knees at the old man's feet and tell him everything that had happened. But he was scared. He was scared, and he felt cut off from the rest of the world, like a prisoner in a dark, windowless dungeon. Still, he had to pretend that everything was all right. So he merely smiled wanly, turned, and began climbing the creaky oak staircase toward his bedroom.

Grampa Dixon rocked back and forth in his rocking chair. He looked thoughtful, and also tense. Suddenly he got up and walked across the room to the doorway that opened into the hall. He stood there a few minutes, peering up at the dark staircase. From the bathroom came the sound of running water. Grampa stepped back into the living room and pulled the sliding door shut. Then he walked over to his smoking stand and picked up the chipped green glass ashtray. He turned it this way and that in the lamplight and examined it as if it were a rare museum object. Then he set the ashtray down and began to pace back and forth on the rug, limping slightly because of his arthritis.

Tap, tap. What was that? Grampa turned toward the bay window and looked. There in the lower part of the window, his nose pressed to the glass, was the professor. He looked like a crabby sort of ghost, peering in. Grampa grinned. He had been expecting the professor to make an appearance. Quickly Grampa limped across the room and pulled back the door. Once more he glanced up at the dark staircase. No sound. Johnny must be in bed now and—probably—sound asleep. Grampa went to the front door and opened it. There stood the professor. He looked as if he had been wading through deep, wet underbrush. The knees of his pants were soiled, and there were sprigs of juniper decorating his coat here and there. His tennis shoes were soaked and caked with mud.

"Come on outside," whispered the professor hoarsely. He pointed back over his left shoulder toward the front yard. "I can't talk in the house. I'd be afraid Johnny would be listening down the hot-air vent or something."

Grampa followed the professor out across the front porch and down the steps. Halfway down the sidewalk the professor turned.

"Okay, this is fine," he hissed. He dug his hand into one of his coat pockets and pulled out a box of Balkan Sobranie cigarettes. Opening it, he took one out and lit it.

"Something is very wrong, Henry," he began as he puffed at his cigarette. "Very wrong indeed. I followed John down to the church, and then from there over across the river to Duston Park."

Grampa's mouth dropped open. "Holy God! What the heck'd he want to go over *there* for?"

The professor grimaced. "Your guess is as good as mine, Henry. But the most disturbing part is yet to come. When he got there, he sat down on a bench. Well, for a while then he just sat there. But all of a sudden he looked up, as if he saw somebody coming. And then, I swear to God, he sat there and had a conversation with somebody who *was not there*!" The professor paused and stared grimly at the ground. "Make something of *that*, if you can!"

Grampa was at a loss for words. He glanced up at the

dark window of Johnny's bedroom, and he shook his head. "My Lord!" he said in a low, somber voice. "What the devil do you think is wrong with him?"

The professor puffed some more at his cigarette, and he made little *hem! hem!* noises in his throat. This meant that he was thinking. "Henry," he said at last, "how long ago was it that his mother died?"

Grampa thought a bit. "It was . . . well, in July of last year. Almost a year ago now."

The professor nodded. "Mm-hmm. And then, right after that, his dad got hauled back into the Air Force, and Johnny got shipped up here to a strange new place, to new surroundings and new . . . new everything."

Grampa looked puzzled. He put his hands on his hips and peered down at the professor over the tops of his glasses. "Rod, what the heck are you tryin' to say?"

The professor gave Grampa a dirty look. "Don't call me Rod. But to answer your question, what I'm trying to say is just this: I think Johnny may be suffering—suffering mentally—because too many bad and upsetting things happened to him in too short a space of time."

Grampa wrinkled up his forehead. He looked very concerned. "You mean . . . you mean you think Johnny's gone *crazy*?"

"No, no, *no!*" snapped the professor, waving his hand impatiently. "I didn't say that! I didn't say that at *all!*" He heaved a deep sigh and, with an effort, controlled his temper. "What I am *trying* to say," he went on through clenched teeth, "is merely that people—even reasonable, sane people like you and me—can go off our trolleys temporarily if bad things happen to us. I don't mean that Johnny is ready for a straitjacket. But he *is* acting a mite peculiar, and he seems to be pretty unhappy. And so I think we'd better get him some help, and get it quick."

"Help?" said Grampa, still mystified. "What kind of help?"

The professor looked exasperated. "Mental help. Henry, you are living in the twentieth century, whether you like it or not. I know that psychiatrists aren't terribly popular yet in America, but I will venture to predict that in ten or twenty years there'll be hordes of them all over the country, making money hand over fist by solving people's problems. But all this is beside the point. We need to do something for Johnny right now. What's the name of your family doctor?"

"Doc Schermerhorn. You know him, don't you?"

The professor frowned. "Hmm. Yes, I know him. He's the one who diagnosed my cousin Bea's brain tumor as bad teeth, shortly after which she died. But I suppose he'll do. Any port in a storm, as they say. All right then: Why don't you get Johnny an appointment with good old Doc Schermerhorn? Explain the problem to the doctor, but don't tell Johnny why you're making him see the doctor. Tell him . . . well, why don't you tell him that you think he needs a checkup. Yes. That's it—a checkup. Meanwhile I'll see if I can figure out something else that might be done. All right?"

Grampa nodded. "All right. And thanks a lot for your help, Rod. You're a real good friend to Johnny."

"Don't mention it. Eventually John may need to see a real psychiatrist. I wish I could recommend one, but I know only one personally, and I wouldn't use him as a shield in a mud-ball fight. See you tomorrow. By the way, if you keep calling me Rod, I'll start calling you Hank. How about that, huh?"

Grampa shrugged helplessly. "But what the heck else can I call you? It's your name, isn't it?"

The professor grinned mischievously. "Call me Randy. My middle name is Random. I was named for Roderick Random, a character in a novel by Tobias Smollett. Good night." He turned abruptly and marched back across the street to his house, humming as he went.

Johnny did not get much sleep that night. He tossed and turned and kept waking up to listen for noises that weren't there. When he arrived in the kitchen for breakfast the next morning, he looked like the walking dead. His eyes were red, and his hair was mussed, and he felt prickly all over. He kept glancing nervously this way and that, as if he expected things to come springing at him out of the corners of the room.

Grampa was sitting at the kitchen table. He was sipping coffee and munching on a piece of toast. He glanced quickly at Johnny and then looked down at his plate. Gramma was over at the stove, stirring the oatmeal she always made for Johnny's breakfast.

"Hi," said Johnny sluggishly, and he slumped into his seat.

"Hi, there," said Gramma without turning around. "Nice morning, eh?"

"Uh-huh," said Johnny tonelessly. Bright sunshine was streaming in through the kitchen window, but it might have been raining or blizzarding for all he cared.

Silence. You could hear the electric clock over the stove buzzing.

"Johnny," said Gramma at last, turning and smiling kindly at him, "we want you to go see our doctor, Doc Schermerhorn."

"Yeah," Grampa added. He coughed to hide his nervousness. "We . . . we think you look kinda under the weather these days, an' so . . . well, we think you oughta have a checkup. We got you an appointment for this mornin', an' we called up the school an' told the sister you was gonna be home t'day, on account of you felt sick. The appointment is at nine o'clock. After you have your breakfast, we can get in the car an' go."

Johnny looked warily at Grampa, and then at Gramma. How much did they know? Had they found the figurine? Did they know about Mr. Beard? He swallowed hard and tried to look healthy and bright-eyed, which under the circumstances was rather difficult.

"Gee," he said, trying to be jaunty, "I don't see what

you guys are all worked up about. I mean, I feel great, I really do!"

This was more than Gramma could stand. She turned around with the bowl of steaming oatmeal in her hands, and she glared at Johnny. "John Dixon!" she exclaimed, indignantly. "That is the *worst* lie I have ever heard in my life! You look like the wreck of the *Hesperus*! I wouldn't be surprised if you was runnin' a fever! So don't sit there with your face hangin' out an' say that you feel all tippy-tip-top an' fine! Lord above!"

Johnny hung his head. Tears came to his eyes, and he bit his lip. Once again he had a strong urge to confess everything, but, as before, his fear held him back. The ring on his finger was like a dynamite bomb strapped to his body. If he told everything, it would go off.

"I . . . I'm sorry," he said in a low, sniffly voice. "I guess I don't feel too good today. I . . . I'd like to go see the doctor."

And so later that morning Johnny went downtown with his grandparents to see Dr. Schermerhorn. Dr. Schermerhorn had an office on the third floor of the First National Bank building on Merrimack Street. Dr. Schermerhorn was a fat, shambly man who chuckled a lot and told very bad jokes. He examined Johnny and announced that there was nothing wrong with him. He suggested that Johnny stay home and rest for a day or two. Gramma and Grampa were not satisfied with this, however. They insisted on talking to the doctor in private, and they told him about the strange things that

Johnny had been doing lately. Dr. Schermerhorn thought a bit, and he hemmed and hawed a bit, and finally he took a pad and a piece of paper and wrote a name and address on it:

Highgaz Melkonian, M.D.
Zero Brattle St.
Cambridge, Mass.

"This guy is a psychiatrist," said Dr. Schermerhorn as he handed the slip of paper to Grampa Dixon. "Now, speaking personally, I don't care very much for head-shrinkers. But it might be worth a try. This guy is as smart as a whip, an' he speaks about sixteen languages. Hypnotizes people too—that's one o' his big techniques. Watch out he don't hypnotize you outa too much money." Dr. Schermerhorn laughed a great deal at his little joke, and he was still chuckling as Gramma and Grampa left his office.

Gramma and Grampa went home and told the professor about their meeting with Dr. Schermerhorn. He listened with great interest and said that in his opinion Dr. Melkonian might be able to help. He added that he himself would pay for any fees that Dr. Melkonian charged. And he would also take care of getting Johnny an appointment with the doctor as soon as he could possibly manage it.

Johnny stayed home for the day. He did picture puzzles and read and listened to the radio. That evening he took some pills that Dr. Schermerhorn had given him, and he slept soundly all night. The next morning he felt much better and was ready to go back to school. But when he got downstairs, he found that he had another doctor's appointment. That morning he was going to go down to Cambridge with the professor. The professor did not tell Johnny that Dr. Melkonian was a psychiatrist. He was afraid that this might scare Johnny off. So he told him that the doctor was a hypnotist. He would help Johnny to relax and sleep soundly at night. Johnny had heard of hypnotists, of course. He had always kind of wanted to be hypnotized, just to see what it was like. So when he got in the car to drive down with the professor, he was a little afraid, but mainly he was eager and curious. In the back of his mind, though, like a dark cloud on the horizon, was the other appointment that he had: at midnight, on the seventeenth of May, in Duston Park. It would be scary, he told himself, but it was something he had to do. At least afterward he would be rid of the ring and the blue figurine. And maybe someday, far in the future, he would sit around and tell his grandchildren about the run-in he had had with a real live ghost.

Later that morning Johnny found himself sitting in a rather luxurious waiting room. There was a red Oriental rug on the floor, and the two big couches had puffy, hissy cushions of chocolate-colored leather. Near the door was a bookcase full of books in green and red morocco leather bindings. The books were about spiritualism and the occult, for the most part. While they waited the professor leafed through the books, and now and then he would say things like "Rubbish—utter rubbish!" or "My God, and people actually *believe* stuff like this!" Eventually the door of the inner office opened, and Dr. Melkonian stepped out. He was about as tall as the professor, and he had jet-black, greasy hair that ran in ripples across his head. His beard was also black, and well trimmed, and his lips were rosy red. He wore a light-gray cutaway and dark-gray pinstriped trousers and a double-breasted waistcoat and an ascot with a pearl stickpin. He looked like somebody who was getting ready to go to a wedding.

"Ah!" he said, nodding politely and smiling. "You're here—good! Please come in."

The professor and Johnny followed Dr. Melkonian into his book-lined inner office. They sat down in two easy chairs, and the doctor sat down behind his desk.

"Now then," said the doctor as he picked up his dagger-shaped letter opener and began to play with it, "what seems to be the trouble?"

The professor explained. He said that Johnny was very nervous and had had trouble sleeping. Dr. Schermerhorn had examined him and had found nothing wrong—nothing physical, that is—and so they had come here, hoping that Dr. Melkonian would be able to give help of a somewhat different sort.

Dr. Melkonian smiled suavely and turned to Johnny. He folded his hands on his desk, sat back, and asked

Johnny a couple of questions. Then he took a pair of collapsible pince-nez glasses out of his desk drawer, opened them up, and peered hard at Johnny through them. Then he got up and walked around to the other side of the desk and stood over Johnny, stroking his beard and sizing Johnny up through the glasses, as if he were going to paint his picture. Finally Dr. Melkonian paced back and forth a bit, and then, halting abruptly, he picked up the beater of a small bronze gong that stood on top of a glazed bookcase. He hit the gong and stood listening as the deep vibrating tones died away. Then he asked the professor to go out into the waiting room and wait.

Time passed. The professor smoked half a pack of Balkan Sobranie cigarettes, and he read quickly through several of the books in the bookcase. Finally the door of the inner office opened, and Dr. Melkonian appeared. He motioned for the professor to come in.

"Please sit down," said the doctor. "Would you care for a cigarette?" He held out a flat gray tin box of Balkan Sobranie cigarettes.

The professor grinned, and he took one. "So you smoke these filthy things too! It's my favorite brand!"

The doctor seemed pleased. "Ah! You are a man of distinction and culture. Of course I could tell that the moment you walked in. You are a professor—an intellectual. I like intellectuals. By the way, in case you are wondering where young John is, he is asleep on a bed in my examining room. I gave him a dose of sodium pentothal to ease him into hypnosis, and he's sleeping off the effects." Dr. Melkonian looked thoughtful and shook his head. "My, my! His case *is* a strange one! I've never handled one quite like it." He paused and looked hard at the professor. "You're a friend of his, aren't you? I mean, you're his special friend, I gather. Isn't that so?"

The professor nodded.

"And," the doctor went on, "you know him pretty well. Eh?"

Again the professor nodded.

"Well, then, tell me: Does he lie much?"

The question was so unexpected that the professor laughed. Then he shook his head. "No," he said firmly. "No. He doesn't lie much. Why do you ask?"

"Because his story's a real doozer, that's why. Actually I would agree with your impression of him. He seems like a pretty truthful kid. And he seems to really believe what he told me when I put him under hypnosis." Dr. Melkonian puffed at his cigarette. He stared at the green desk blotter and drew circles on it with his finger. Then he looked up suddenly. "He thinks he's met the ghost of a priest who used to live in your city."

The professor's mouth dropped open. Then he slapped his forehead with the palm of his hand. "Oh, *no*! Good gravy, I should have *known*! This is all my fault! I told him that stupid, idiotic tale about Father Baart, and he *believed* it!"

Dr. Melkonian gave the professor an irritated glance. "My dear sir, this is more than believing a story. Johnny has been having delusions—hallucinations. He actually thinks he's met with this ghost. And the ghost gave him a magic ring, and there's a blue statue mixed in with the whole mess somehow. What he told me just sort of came tumbling out, and it was all a bit confused. Anyway, he thinks he has to show up in this park next . . . next Friday, I think it is. If he doesn't, then bad things will happen to him. The ghost will kill him."

The professor looked worried. An odd thought had come into his mind. He examined the burning end of his cigarette and wrinkled up his nose. "You don't think . . ." he said hesitantly, "you don't think there might possibly *be* a ghost, do you?"

Dr. Melkonian looked at the professor incredulously for an instant. Then he burst into loud, uproarious laughter. "Oh, that's a *good* one!" he exclaimed, still laughing. "A *ghost*? Good night, man, what century are you living in? Ghosts went out when the electric light was invented! Ha-*haaa*! Ghosts! My, how you do run on!"

Dr. Melkonian went on chortling. Meanwhile the professor folded his arms across his chest and glowered crabbily. The psychiatrist's laughter died away when he saw the way the professor was looking at him. He picked up his letter opener and began nervously fiddling with it. It was almost as if he were going to use it to defend himself in case the professor sprang at him.

"Now, listen," said the professor, still glaring fiercely, "I am a cranky old man, and I don't enjoy being made fun of. If you think ghosts are such a great big fat joke, then what are all those ghost books doing out in your waiting room? Eh?"

Dr. Melkonian smiled and waved his hand airily. "Oh, they are there to amuse my patients. If you're a psychiatrist, you get a lot of nuts as patients, and nutty people often believe in ghosts. But you don't seem nutty to me. That's why I was surprised at what you said."

"I'm not nutty," said the professor through his teeth. "I'm as sane as you are, and possibly even saner."

"All right, all right, you're sane!" muttered the doctor irritably. "Let's change the subject! I believe you told me over the phone that Johnny lost his mother recently. Is that correct?"

"Yes. And, in a way, he also lost his father when he was hauled back into the Air Force to be a jet pilot. And these two things, to my way of thinking, may have—"

"Yes, yes!" cut in Dr. Melkonian with an impatient gesture. "I was about to say something like that myself. It seems to me likely that Johnny's delusions may be caused by the losses and dislocations that have occurred in his life recently." The doctor coughed self-importantly and picked up a pen. He began to doodle on the green blotter. "Now, what I would recommend," he went on, "is this: First I think we should explain to him, as best we can, that his mind has been playing tricks on him. Then I think you should go with him to that park—what was its name? Dusty Park? Is that right?"

"Duston Park," said the professor. "It's named for— but never mind. Go on."

"Ah, yes. Duston Park. Well, I think you should go there with him. He should keep his 'appointment' with this idiotic nonexistent ghost. Then, when no ghost shows up, and nothing hideous or nasty happens to him, he'll feel better. After that, as soon as school is out, I think he ought to be gotten out of town. Can his grandparents afford to take him on a vacation?"

The professor frowned and shook his head sadly. "No. They're as poor as church mice—poorer even. They—" He stopped because a thought had struck him. He snapped his fingers. "By God!" he exclaimed. "But *I* can take him on a trip! I'd *love* to! How about that? Eh? Eh?"

Dr. Melkonian grinned and nodded approvingly. "I think that would be just peachy-dandy. After the experience he's had—or thinks he's had—he needs to get away. Good. Excellent. I'm glad you'll be able to take him. Oh, by the way, I have something that belongs to him. A ring. It was on his finger, and he told me—under hypnosis—that the ghost of Father Baart had given him the ring. There's a letter B under the stone, and I suppose you could imagine that that stood for *Baart*. At any rate, according to Johnny the ghost had told him that he couldn't take the ring off. He would die if he did. Well, I took it off while he was asleep, and needless to say, he didn't die." Dr. Melkonian paused and dug his hand into his coat pocket. He fished out the ring and handed it to the professor. "Here. Do you know anything about it?"

The professor took the ring and turned it back and

forth, examining it. The small yellow stone sparkled fitfully in the lamplight. "No," he said slowly. "No, I don't know a blessed thing about it. I saw it on Johnny's finger one day, and I asked him where he had gotten it, and he said that his grandfather had given it to him. Then I asked his grandfather about it, and he said that Johnny had told him that *I* gave it to him. And from all this I concluded that Johnny had gotten the ring in some weird way and didn't want to tell anyone how." The professor flipped the ring up in the air and caught it. "I can't imagine that he stole it. I mean, he's not the thieving kind, and anyway, it doesn't look like it'd be worth stealing. The stone looks like a piece of bottle glass, and the body of the ring seems to have been made out of a rusty—"

At this point the door of the examining room opened, and Johnny came stumbling out. His hair was mussed, and his glasses were stuck on crooked, and his eyes were heavy with sleep.

"Hi," he said shyly. "Can I come out now?"

Dr. Melkonian asked Johnny to sit down in one of the easy chairs. And then he and the professor had a long talk with him. They explained to Johnny that Mr. Beard —otherwise known as Father Baart—was just a figment of his imagination. When Johnny heard this, he was shocked and bewildered. And then he got angry.

"Whaddaya mean, I didn't see him!" Johnny burst

out. "He was right there in front of me, just like you are!"

Dr. Melkonian smiled blandly and folded his hands on the desk. "Yes, yes, young man," he said smoothly. "You saw him, all right—only he wasn't there. He existed only in your mind. You've heard of mirages, haven't you? Well, Mr. Beard was like a mirage. You've been through a great deal of sorrow lately, young man. And sorrow can make us do strange things and . . . and *see* strange things. Please try to understand. I'm not saying that you're crazy or that you are lying. I'm merely trying to help you understand what happened to you."

Johnny was stunned. He didn't know what to say. "But . . . but . . . ." he stammered, "he . . . he gave me a ring. . . ." Johnny looked down at his left hand. The ring was gone! Immediately he felt panic. What would happen to him now?

The professor held up the ring. "Dr. Melkonian took this off your finger while you were asleep," he said gently. "And don't worry—you're not going to die. There's no ghost, and no curse on you, or on that stupid blue hunk of crockery. So relax. Everything's going to be all right."

Johnny was not so sure about that. Dr. Melkonian and the professor talked very seriously with him for a long time. They argued and wheedled and were terribly logical as they tried to prove to Johnny that the ghost was just imaginary. Johnny resisted. Like most people, he resented it when somebody told him that he had not seen something that he really thought he had seen.

"But what about the ring?" he said insistently. "I mean, I didn't make it up. It's right there on the desk!"

"I know," said Dr. Melkonian patiently. "But you may have found the ring somewhere. Maybe you found it in the church that night when you thought you ran into Mr. Beard for the first time. Don't get me wrong. I'm not accusing you of lying. Mr. Beard must have seemed very, very real to you, as real as the professor here, or as me. But hallucinations are that way. You can't tell them from the real thing—you really, truly can't!"

Johnny was beginning to feel desperate. "But he talked to me! I *heard* him!"

Dr. Melkonian was not impressed. "Auditory illusions are common," he said. "Haven't you ever imagined that you heard somebody calling your name?"

"Okay, okay! But what about the time I told you about, when the ring flashed and this big wind knocked Eddie Tompke for a loop? How about that, huh?"

"Ring stones flash in the sunlight sometimes," said the doctor smoothly. "And as for the sudden wind . . . well, when you live in New England, you learn to expect things like that. The sea causes violent and unexpected changes in the weather."

"But Eddie was scared! He really was!"

Dr. Melkonian smiled faintly. "I'm sure he was. Something startling like that, a wind strong enough to knock you off your pins . . . well, it would have scared me too.

But it's a *natural* occurrence, not a supernatural one! Can't you see that?"

And so it went. After an hour of this sort of thing Johnny was beginning to have doubts about what he had seen and heard. He was still not entirely convinced, but he did have doubts. To tell the truth, he *wanted* to have doubts. If Father Baart was imaginary, that meant that he was not being threatened with death and destruction. On the other hand, the whole experience had been so real, so very real. Johnny's mind began to whirl. Nothing made sense anymore. Was Dr. Melkonian real? Was the professor real? Was *anything* real?

After the session in Dr. Melkonian's office Johnny rode home to Duston Heights in the professor's car. On the way the professor asked Johnny if he would like to go on a little trip with him after school was over. He explained that they would be going up into the White Mountains to sight-see and hike around, and maybe even do a little mountain climbing. Johnny was delighted by this idea. He had seen pictures of the White Mountains of New Hampshire, but he had never actually been up there on a visit. The trip sounded great. But now his mind shifted to a totally different subject: What was he going to do about the meeting that he was supposed to have—or wasn't supposed to have—with Mr. Beard in Duston Park next Friday night? The professor, glancing sideways, saw the look on Johnny's face, and he read his thoughts.

"Are you worried about your midnight rendezvous?" he asked with a slight smile.

Johnny nodded glumly. "Yeah. What . . . whaddaya think I oughta do?"

The professor's smile got broader and more confident. "Dr. Melkonian and I discussed this," he said briskly, "and we think that you should keep this so-called appointment. I'll go with you, and if a ghost shows up . . . well, I've always kind of had a hankering to see one. Are you game? Are you still willing to go?"

Johnny nodded. And so that was settled.

When they got back to Fillmore Street, the professor had a little talk with the Dixons. He explained to them as well as he could what Dr. Melkonian had said about Johnny and his problems. They were suspicious because they didn't like psychiatrists. They thought psychiatrists were like witch doctors, and they also thought that only crazy people believed in the things that psychiatrists said. But they were glad to hear that Johnny was not seriously ill, or ready for the insane asylum. And they thought that the trip to the White Mountains was really a very wonderful idea.

Several days passed. One afternoon when the Dixons were out shopping, the professor sneaked over and took away the blue figurine and the hollow book that held it. He had told Johnny that he was going to do this, and Johnny agreed that it was probably a good idea. Meanwhile Johnny went about his usual routine. He felt much, much better than he had felt in a long time. He slept soundly at night, and he did not hear any strange noises. He felt as if a great weight had been lifted from his shoulders. Naturally he was still a bit worried about Friday night. He did not know what was going to happen—not really. But, he reminded himself, the ring was gone from his finger, and he was still among the living. That was an encouraging thought, to say the least.

Friday night came, and it was pouring rain outside. The professor, umbrella in hand, met Johnny at the front door of his house at a quarter to twelve. Off they went, through the wind and wet, and finally they arrived in Duston Park. They stood around by Hannah Duston's statue and waited. The streetlight burned placidly, and the bronze Hannah hovered as menacingly as ever. The rain pelted down and made a racket on the stiff cloth of the professor's umbrella. Across the street the columned church loomed ghostly and white, thrusting its tall spire up into the night sky. Time passed. Fifteen minutes, half an hour. Nobody came.

The professor unbuttoned his raincoat, reached into his jacket pocket, and pulled out his watch. He glanced at it, sniffed, and looked around.

"Well," he said dryly, "Shakespeare would say that this was a night when the sheeted dead might squeak and gibber in the streets. But they ain't out, and on a night like this I don't blame them. No, sir, I don't blame them at all." He put his watch back in his pocket and peered owlishly around. Then he folded his arms, leered jauntily, and began to whistle. It was an old tune, "The Ghost of John." After he had whistled it through once, he sang softly:

> Have you seen the ghost of John?
> Long white bones and the flesh all gone?
> Oh, ooooh-ohhhhh!
> Wouldn't it be chilly with no skin on?

Johnny was not in such a jolly mood. He would have liked to be, but he couldn't manage it. He was staring intently at the great mass of shadow on the right side of the Unitarian church. Mr. Beard had walked out of that darkness last Saturday night. Try as he might, Johnny just couldn't persuade himself that Mr. Beard was imaginary. Yet the professor had told him that Mr. Beard didn't exist. Dr. Melkonian had told him this too. And now, here in the park, the professor was singing silly songs and making fun of ghostly fears. Johnny asked himself why he couldn't let go of his lingering fear and be cheerful too.

The rain kept pouring down. Now the wind began to blow, and Johnny felt rain slashing across his legs. A hard gust hit them, and the professor staggered sideways.

"Drat!" growled the professor as he pulled the umbrella back over their heads. He turned and looked at Johnny, who was still peering anxiously this way and that. "Look, John," he said in a more gentle tone, "we ought to be getting on home. Nothing is going to happen here, believe me. Nothing except that we might go to sleep on our feet. I'm an old geezer, and these late hours are not for the likes of me." He yawned hugely and flapped his hand against his mouth. "Let's head for home. How about it? Eh? Are you with me?"

Johnny nodded. They trotted off down the long sidewalk that ran diagonally across the little park. They paused at the curb, and a car whooshed past. Its taillights stained the pavement red. As they started across the street Johnny glanced back, one more time, over his shoulder. Nobody there. Why couldn't he be calm? Why couldn't he heave a deep sigh of relief? Well, he couldn't. Johnny felt nothing but foreboding, the fear of someone who is waiting for something to happen.

CHAPTER TEN

On a bright but chilly day in June, Johnny was sitting in the front seat of the professor's mud-spattered maroon Pontiac. They were zooming along on U.S. 3, which winds north into the White Mountains. Johnny felt happy. He was eating Planters peanuts out of a can, and he was gaping this way and that. They were in the mountains, in the mountains at last. For some time they had driven through rather blah, ordinary, slightly hilly country. Then in the distance Johnny began to see rumpled blue shapes. Now they were among those shapes. Great humped masses rose above the road. Trees marched up the sides of the mountains or bristled on their ridges—pines and maples for the most part, with here and there the startling white fork of a birch tree.

Crags and horns of stone topped some of the mountains or jutted from their sides. Here and there the masses of trees would part, and dizzyingly high on the side of a mountain, Johnny would see a slanting green pasture and wonder if animals or people could ever get to such a place.

Johnny was entranced. Growing up on Long Island, he had never seen mountains, except in pictures and in movies. Now here he was.

The professor darted a quick glance at his companion. "Well, are you enjoying yourself?" he asked.

Johnny nodded. He was sublimely happy. The sense of foreboding that had hung over him for days had finally passed away.

He had had three more sessions with Dr. Melkonian, and finally, after a lot of thought, he had become convinced—well, more or less convinced—that Mr. Beard was a product of his imagination. "Insufficient grievement" was the phrase Dr. Melkonian had used when he was explaining Johnny's problem. It was a pretty highfalutin term, but what it meant in plain English was that Johnny had not cried enough over the death of his mother. This, together with the other changes that had taken place in his life, had caused Johnny to see and hear things that weren't there. All these horrors and hallucinations were behind him now. The "magic" ring was in his desk drawer. The blue figurine was over at the professor's house. And right now the only question in Johnny's mind was, when do we eat?

He asked it aloud: "Hey, Professor! When are we gonna eat?"

The professor smiled secretively. "When we get there. And if you want to know where 'there' is, I won't tell you. So shut up and look at the scenery and munch your peanuts."

Johnny sighed. They had been driving since eight in the morning, and now it was one thirty. Even with the peanuts his stomach was rumbling. But he knew the professor well enough to know that pestering wouldn't help. He would just have to wait.

They drove on, through Franconia Notch, a gap in the mountains, and into the little village of Franconia. Then they came to the Gale River, a cheerful, sparkly little stream that ran noisily over a bed of smooth white stones. They crossed a green iron bridge that had flower boxes hanging on it, and they crawled up and down some steep hills. At last they came to a place high up in the mountains where a sprawly white farmhouse stood. Next to it was a building that looked like a large shed. It was covered with shaggy bark, and tacked to the front of the building were crooked letters that spelled POLLY'S PANCAKE PARLOR. Johnny and the professor went in, and they gorged themselves. They ordered the All You Can Eat Waffle Special, which meant that the waitress kept bringing you buckwheat or corn-meal waffles until you couldn't stuff in one more single delicious syrup-soaked crumb. Then they stumbled outside to stare at the Presidential Range, Mount Washington, Mount Jefferson, and the others. They sat on a green bench for a while and talked while an enormous elm tree rustled overhead. And then they climbed back into the car and drove on to do more sight-seeing.

At the end of the day, tired and sunburned and happy, the two travelers found themselves standing outside a motel called Hag View Cottages. It was really a rather nice motel, in spite of its sinister name. Each cottage was a miniature house, with a steep green shingled roof and a little brick fireplace and a teeny-tiny screened porch. The name of the place came from the big tourist attraction in the area: the Hag. The Hag was a curious rock formation high up on the side of Hellbent Mountain. If you looked at the mass of shelving rock from the correct angle, you saw the face of an old witch. People came from all over the country to gape at the Hag and take pictures of it and buy souvenirs in the various gift shops in the area. Everything for miles around was named for the Hag: there were the Hag Kumfy Kabins, there was the Haggis Baggis Bar and Grill, there was Hag Lake, and there was Hagtooth Harry's Bear Ranch, featuring trained bears that did all sorts of fascinating tricks. Johnny and the professor had visited all the attractions and had seen the bears and had prowled through gift shops. They had slogged along wilderness trails and had sipped water from mountain streams. Now they were tired, just incredibly tired, and all they wanted to do—for the time being—was *rest*.

"Nice evening, eh?" said the professor. He gazed

placidly off across the road at Hellbent Mountain, which towered above them, a massive, dark presence. The late sunlight touched the horn of rock at the top with reddish fire. Birds rustled in a nearby tree, settling themselves for the night. In the deep blue of the evening sky a black bar of cloud hung.

Johnny was about to say something by way of response when the professor let out a loud exclamation.

"Drat! Double drat with cream and sugar! I'm out of cigarettes!" He held up the black Balkan Sobranie box and flapped the lid. "Now, where am I going to get cigarettes at this time of night? Hmmm? Tell me that!"

"How about the gift shop across the road?" Johnny suggested. "I thought I saw some cigarettes in there. Up in front, behind the cash register."

The professor was amused. He had almost gotten thrown out of the gift shop across the road. He had been criticizing the souvenirs, laughing at them and calling them "trash" and "rubbish." And he had done his criticizing in a rather loud voice. The lady who ran the shop, a persnickety sort of woman with chains on her glasses and a permanent frown on her face, had glowered at him a lot; finally she had told him that if he didn't like her stuff, he could keep his opinions to himself.

"Hmh!" snorted the professor. He squinted across the road. "My eyes are not good for distance, John. Tell me, does it look like the place is still open?"

Johnny nodded. "I think so. I mean, the light in the window is still on."

The professor heaved a deep pull-yourself-together-and-prepare-for-the-worst sigh. "Very well," he said resignedly. "If I must, I must. If you hear a loud crash, that will be the lady breaking one of her cheap souvenir lamps over my noggin. I'll be back in a minute." And he set out for the road with quick, purposeful strides.

Johnny watched him go. He felt a sudden pang of fear, fear of being left alone. Then he laughed. Imaginary ghosts, Father Baart, hallucinations—all that was in the past. He was okay now. Nothing could hurt him. He turned and started walking back toward the cottage, whistling softly to himself. As he went his footsteps crunched on the gravel path. Some of the cottages were lit; others were not. Out in front of one a car was parked, and a man was lifting luggage out of the trunk. Johnny walked on. Even though all the cottages looked alike, the one he and the professor were staying in was not hard to find. It was the one on the very end. Ah. Here he was. The yellow insect light burned over the door. And the professor had left one of the lamps burning, so the place had a homey look. Johnny looked up at the darkening sky, took a deep breath, and went inside.

But he had barely stepped through the door when he had the sudden, creepy, alarming feeling that something was wrong. What was it? He looked nervously this way and that. His suitcase lay open on his bed, just as he had left it. The professor's shirts were draped over the back of the armchair, but there was nothing frightening about that. *What could it be?* What had upset him?

And then he noticed. There was a small black book lying open on the bureau.

Johnny stared. He knew what the book was: It was a Gideon Bible. There is a society called the Gideons, and they put Bibles in hotel and motel rooms all over America. The professor had explained all this to Johnny when they found the Bible in the top drawer of the bureau. But then the professor had put the Bible back in the drawer. Johnny remembered seeing him do this. So what was the book doing out where it was?

Johnny drew closer to the bureau. The book was propped open with one of the professor's silver-backed hairbrushes. Johnny saw that the Bible was open to the twelfth chapter of Saint Paul's Epistle to the Romans. And he saw that part of the nineteenth verse had been underlined in red ink:

Vengeance is mine; I will repay, saith the Lord.

Johnny stared. The words seemed to squirm and writhe before his eyes. He felt cold all over. Those words were well known to him: They were part of the warning note that Father Baart had put into the black book. Johnny felt creepy, cold panic growing in his mind. Everything had been so peaceful, so happy all day. He had been having so much fun, and now . . . well, these words were like a lump of ice that had been placed suddenly in his hand. He was frightened and startled. And he felt very alone.

When the professor got back to the cottage, he was smoking a Murad, which was like a Balkan Sobranie only smellier. Slam went the screen door. The professor looked vaguely around, and he was brought up short by the sight of Johnny. Johnny was sitting, rigid and deathly silent, on the edge of his bed. It didn't take too many smarts to tell that Johnny was scared out of his wits.

"My God!" exclaimed the professor, taking the cigarette out of his mouth. "What on *earth* is the matter with you?"

Johnny didn't answer. He raised a trembling hand and pointed toward the bureau. The professor gaped at Johnny uncomprehendingly. Then he stepped quickly to the bureau and examined the book. Still, the professor was mystified.

"I don't get it," he said, turning to Johnny again. "I mean, is this some kind of game, or what? Did you underline these words?"

With an effort Johnny managed to speak. "I . . . I didn't do . . . it. The . . . the ghost must've."

"Oh, ghost my *foot*!" exclaimed the professor angrily. "I thought we were through with ghosts!" Immediately the professor was sorry that he had exploded at Johnny. He saw the hangdog, miserable look on Johnny's face, and he cursed himself for having such a rotten temper.

"I'm sorry, John," he said gently. "I shouldn't have snapped at you like that. I can see that you're upset—very upset. But all I see here are some words underlined in red. Now, they're certainly threatening words, but . . ."

The professor's voice trailed away. Suddenly he had remembered. "Oh, *I* see! And you think . . . no, no, it's just not true! These words here, about vengeance, they're really rather famous words. And people are always underlining passages in Bibles. Especially Gideon Bibles. They're kind of . . . well, they're common property, like the soap and the towels in the bathroom. This is nothing to get upset about, really it isn't!"

Again Johnny tried to speak. He was so upset that it was hard for him, but he managed it. "But . . . Professor! The . . . the book was propped open there when I came in. It wasn't like that before!"

The professor frowned. He bit his lip and thought. "Hmm. Well then, if what you say is true, this is a serious matter. But it doesn't have anything to do with spooks and specters. No. There's some fruitcake on the loose, some nut who runs into motel rooms and leaves threatening notes. Don't you see? That's what's happened."

Johnny tried hard to convince himself that the professor's explanation was the right one. While he was struggling with his thoughts the professor went over to the door and peered out into the night.

"I should've locked this door when we went out," he muttered. "But I didn't think there'd be anything to worry about way up here. Well, I'll lock the door tonight, and put the chain on too. Will that make you feel better?"

Johnny nodded. He was calmer now. The panic he had felt before was draining away. "Are you sure it's just some nutty guy?" he said at last.

The professor chuckled. "No. No, I'm not sure. It might be some nutty woman. But whoever it is, it's a flesh-and-blood kook, and not a ghostly one. Get Father Baart out of your mind, *please*, and let's settle down to a game of chess before we hit the sack. How about it? Eh?"

Johnny smiled and nodded. The professor went to his suitcase and got out his peg chess set. He set the game up on a little low table and moved the lamp on the bureau over so they could see to play. Johnny got a stool to sit on, and the professor perched on the edge of his bed. The professor lit another Murad, and Johnny ate some of the maple-flavored chocolate creams that he had bought earlier in the day. They started moving pieces, and the game got under way.

The first game went to the professor. He used the Nimzo-Indian Defense, which Johnny had not yet learned to overcome. But Johnny came roaring back in the second game, and halfway through he was up by two pawns, a bishop, and a knight. Then fatigue set in. It had been a long, tiring day, and now Johnny was feeling the effects. His eyelids kept closing, and his head began to sag forward. The professor was sleepy too. He started to yawn, and he yawned and he yawned. Finally he burst out laughing.

Johnny blinked. "What's so funny?" he asked sluggishly.

"Us!" said the professor, grinning. "We're both so socked that we can hardly stay awake, and yet we keep hacking away at each other in this game as if we were Nimzovich and Alekhine. Let's call it a day, eh? I'll put the set up on the bureau, and we can finish the slaughter tomorrow. What d'you say? Hmm?"

Johnny thought this was a great idea. He went into the bathroom and brushed his teeth and got into his pajamas. The sheets felt icy cold on his feet when he climbed into bed, but they soon felt warmer. He stretched his weary legs out, and the feeling of relaxation was delicious. Johnny sighed happily. The little window over his head was open, and through it he could hear the pines hissing in the wind. Across the room he could see a tiny red dot of fire as the professor smoked his last cigarette of the day. Soon he too would be in bed asleep. Johnny felt himself sinking down, down, down into warm furry darkness. His eyes closed, and he was asleep.

Night lay over the little cluster of green-roofed cottages. Now dark clouds came rushing in to cover the stars, and it rained. Wet drops pattered on the slanted roofs and on the gravel path. It rained for half an hour, a heavy pelting downpour. Then the clouds, driven by a strong wind, blew on past over the ragged top of Hell-bent Mountain, and the stars shone down once more. Inside the cabin Johnny and the professor slept on. The chain lock and the sliding steel bolt held the door fast. But what was this? A tiny tinkling sound, and the chain fell from its groove. Now the bolt moved slowly, silently back. And the door of the cabin opened. A dark hunched shape stepped inside. Its body was a mass of shadows, but its face was lit by a pale, trembling light. The face was that of an old man with a heavy, over-hanging forehead, a jutting chin, a hawkish nose, and deep-set, burning eyes. Long sheaves of whitish hair hung down from the balding dome of the head. And the smile on the man's curled lips was evil and unearthly.

The shape paused just inside the door. It turned this way and that, as if doubtful about what to do next. Then it raised a shadowy hand, and suddenly, on Johnny's pillow, there appeared a yellow dot of light. It was the ring, the ring made from the bent nail. It had been locked up, safe and sound, in Johnny's bureau. But it was here now. Johnny slept on, but his hand crawled up onto the pillow, inching slowly forward, till the third finger of his left hand was thrust through the hollow circle of the ring. And now Johnny sat up. His face was lit by a pale light, and though his eyes were open, he did not seem to be awake. Slowly, moving stiffly and mechanically like a robot, he stood up, and began walking across the floor toward the door. The dark hunched form moved away, out through the open doorway, and Johnny followed.

CHAPTER ELEVEN

The professor slept on, but his sleep was uneasy. He was tossing and turning and moaning, and muttering words aloud from time to time. The professor was dreaming, and in his dream he was a boy again, and he was back in the little white schoolhouse where he had learned his lessons long, long ago. Up in the front of the room was his old teacher, Miss Vary. She was wearing her usual floor-length dress and stiff starched blouse with ruffles at the cuffs. On her head was a bun of gray hair, and on her face was a frown. She was frowning because young Roddy Childermass could not answer the question she had asked him. To make things easier, she had even written the answer on the blackboard. But he couldn't read the answer. It was all blurry and out of focus. Now

Miss Vary, her lips barely moving, asked the question again: *How could . . . Johnny . . . Dixon . . .*

"Yes, yes!" muttered the professor in his sleep. "How could Johnny Dixon *what*?"

But Miss Vary wouldn't tell him. She wouldn't repeat the rest of the question. Young Roddy asked her again; he pleaded tearfully, but she still refused. The professor thrashed back and forth in his bed, muttering and cursing. *How could . . . how could . . . how could Johnny . . .*

Suddenly the professor sat up. He was groggy but awake. And now, to his astonishment, he found himself thinking about something that he had never thought about before. He thought about the name Beard. Mr. Beard. That was the name of the man Johnny claimed he had met in the church. This was the man who had —supposedly—turned into the ghost of Father Baart. The professor was a learned man, and he knew several languages. He asked himself what the German word for beard was. *Bart*, that was what it was. There was a similar word in Dutch, *baard*. But Johnny didn't know German or Dutch. How on earth, then, how on earth had he hit upon a name that meant the same as . . .

The professor was wide awake now. Wide awake, and frightened. He fumbled for the lamp and turned it on. He found his glasses and shoved them onto his face. When he looked across the room he saw that Johnny was gone.

In an instant the professor was on his feet. He was pulling on his pants, pulling them on over his pajama bottoms. Now he was putting on his tennis shoes and lacing them up. He rushed to his suitcase, unsnapped it, and took out his flashlight. Cursing and growling to himself, he hurried to the door and yanked it open. Outside, the wind had died down, but the sky was overcast. Thunder rumbled in the distance—a storm was brewing in the mountains. The professor snapped on his flashlight and played the beam this way and that. Beyond the gravel path was long grass. A matted track had been beaten down through the middle of the grass. That had to be the route that Johnny had taken. The professor moved forward cautiously, eyes to the ground. The grass, slick with rain, squished under his feet. Now he was at the edge of the highway. Quickly he looked to the right and to the left. No cars. He raced across.

On the other side he stopped to pick up the trail again. As it turned out, there was no problem about that. The shoulder of the road was muddy from the rain, and there were tracks in the mud. They were the tracks of a boy's bare feet, and they were the only tracks around. *Good!* said the Professor to himself. *Stay on the muddy ground, for God's sake!* Setting his jaw grimly, he plodded on behind the footprints.

Before long the professor was swinging along on one of the trails that ran up the side of Hellbent Mountain. Luckily the White Mountains were low, humped mountains, and they could be climbed by anyone who could set one foot in front of the other. The White Cross was one of Hellbent Mountain's easier trails. Not that this mattered much to the professor. He was a tough, wiry little man who walked several miles each day and exercised with dumbbells. And in the mood he was in right now, he could have tramped up the side of the Empire State Building. He had—as the saying goes—the bit between his teeth.

Onward and upward. As he climbed the professor kept checking for footprints. When the trail ran over muddy ground, he had no problem. But for long stretches the trail was rocky. Nevertheless the professor did not falter. He marched grimly on, hoping that he would pick up the muddy tracks again. And he always did. But as he went he kept thinking: *Where is he going?* and *Is there anyone with him?* There was only one set of tracks— Johnny's tracks—but if the professor's suspicions were correct, Johnny might have company, company that left no tracks on the ground. He plodded on.

Up and up and up. Higher and higher, over rocks and roots and logs. The thunder was rumbling louder, and now and then lightning would flash off to the right or to the left. Drops of rain pattered among the leaves. *If there is a ghost, and he has dragged me out on a night like this, I'll brain him!* The professor said this to himself, grumbling as he climbed. He said this and things like it to keep up his courage. For to tell the truth, there was a cold pool of fear in his heart. He didn't know what he would find when he reached the end of the trail.

Finally the professor came to a place where the White Cross Trail met another trail, a rocky trail that ran off to the right, and to the left. Heaving a weary sigh, the professor stopped. He was beginning to get tired. He had been climbing for an hour, and his legs felt rubbery. His feet felt like they were going to fall off, and his shirt was wringing wet with sweat. "Ohhhh . . . *Gawwwwwd*!" said the professor, and he took off his glasses. He cleaned them with his handkerchief and put them back on again. Before him were two signs. One pointed off to the right. It said:

TO THE WHIMBY SCENIC OVERLOOK

The other pointed off to the left. It said:

TO THE ANGEL SCENIC VIEW

Tacked to the bottom part of this sign was a rain-spotted piece of cardboard. A message had been scrawled on it in ink. The ink was runny, but the message could still be read: Danger. *Rockslide.*

"Oh, great!" muttered the professor. "Rockslide! But have the rocks slid, or are they getting ready to slide? It would be nice to know which." Still grumbling, he played the beam of the flashlight back and forth over the trail. Lots of rocks, and some tough, knotty roots, but not much dirt to leave tracks in. The professor's heart sank. How would he know which way to go?

And then he saw something. Off to the left a root stuck up out of a clump of stones. And caught on the end of the root was a ragged patch of black cloth. The professor pounced on the cloth and ripped it away from the root.

He held it up, but then his nostrils twitched, and a shudder of disgust ran through his body. The cloth smelled. It smelled of mold, and of things worse than mold. With a quick twitch of his hand the professor threw the piece of cloth to the ground. At least he knew the way to go now.

The path curved around to the left, and the professor followed it, head down, flashlight beam constantly playing back and forth. There were no more tracks, but he had decided that this had to be the way. It was very dark. He couldn't see a thing beyond the pale circle cast by the flashlight's beam. He did notice, however, that the trail was getting narrower. And for some reason—he didn't know exactly why—he had the feeling that the ground was dropping away on the left. Finally he stopped and flashed his light to the right. A beetling, shelving rock wall rose above him. He flashed the light to the left, and he gasped. He was aiming his light out into nothingness. Now everything was clear—altogether too clear. He was on a very narrow path that skirted the edge of a precipice. How far was the drop? It was impossible to say—the beam of his flashlight didn't reach that far. Then thunder rumbled, and lightning leaped from the clouds above. The professor saw, for a split second, the glimmering surface of a lake. It was so far below that it looked about as big as his hand. The professor closed his eyes and swallowed hard. He was afraid of heights. High places gave him attacks of dizziness. But he gritted his teeth and said to himself a line from

Shakespeare that had always given him courage: "Before my body I throw my warlike shield. Lay on, Macduff, and damned be he that first cries hold, enough!" Then he began to pick his way forward again.

More lightning. More thunder. By the fitful pale flashes the professor caught glimpses, now and then, of where the path was going. It seemed to be winding up the eastern face of the mountain. Most of Hellbent Mountain was covered with trees. But the eastern side was a great shattered wall of stone three thousand feet high. Far above the professor's head, in the darkness, were the rocks that formed the face of the Hag. Not that he was terribly interested in scenic rock formations—not right at this moment, thank you. He was just hoping that the trail would hold out. And while he was hoping and wishing and worrying about Johnny, he saw, ahead of him, a glimmering yellow square. It was a wooden sign on a post. The sign said:

NO TRAIL BEYOND THIS POINT

The professor stopped. He inched closer to the sign and played the flashlight beam out into the darkness beyond. Immediately he saw what had happened. A rock slide had wiped out part of the trail. There was a little, narrow, wispy trail left, a ledge about a foot wide. If you were a mountain goat, you would have no trouble bounding along it. The professor's heart sank. Was this it, then? Was this as far as he could go? He tried to imagine himself picking his way along that narrow, bumpy lip of rock. Below, the vast empty darkness gaped. The professor shuddered. As he stood there he was in an agony of indecision. What should he do? What *could* he do?

And then the lightning flashed. Far ahead he saw something.

The trail—what was left of it—straggled along the mountain face to a wide, flat patch, a little grassy lookout that hung over the precipice. And when the lightning flashed, the professor saw two figures standing in this place.

"Oh, God!" said the professor, and he clenched his teeth and closed his eyes. He opened his eyes and began to pray. And as he prayed he crept forward out past the sign to the narrow rocky ledge. He shut off his flashlight, stuck it in his hip pocket, and stepped out into blackness. Splaying his body against the rough rock wall, he began to sidle along. The right side of his head scraped against the stone, and as he went his lips moved constantly. He was saying one of the prayers he had learned as a boy:

St. Michael the Archangel, defend us in the hour of battle. Be our safeguard against the malice and snares of the Devil. Rebuke him we humbly pray, and do Thou O Prince of the Heavenly Host, by the power of God, thrust into Hell Satan and all the other evil spirits that wander about the world seeking the ruin of souls . . .

) 163 (

On crept the professor, inch by inch. He was in an ecstasy of terror. He hardly knew who he was or what he was doing. Horrible thoughts came into his mind. He kept having the awful, insane urge to throw himself backward over the ledge. His temples throbbed, and his glasses steamed up. His body was soaked with sweat. A flake of rock crumbled away under the pressure of his foot. He heard it clatter down, down into the void. Now he imagined that the rock wall was expanding and contracting, like a bellows. It would heave him over no matter what he did. He said the St. Michael prayer again, and the Our Father and the Hail Mary and several Glory Be to the Fathers. Slowly . . . slowly . . . had he reached the wide place yet? In the dark how would he know? Yes, how would he know? *That's a problem we haven't worked out yet*, the professor said to himself, and he began to giggle madly. Then he began to feel like throwing up. Inch by inch . . . inch by inch. . . .

The lightning flashed. He was inching along over solid grassy ground.

He had made it. The sick taste of vomit was in his throat, and he was shuddering, shuddering uncontrollably. But he had made it. And now the professor pulled himself together. He felt his old comfortable rage returning. Where was his blasted flashlight? It was in his hip pocket, where he had put it. He pulled it out and snapped it on. There in the middle of the grassy space stood Johnny. His arms were folded over his chest, and his eyes were closed. The corners of his mouth were curved up into an awful corpselike smile, and on his finger the yellow stone of the ring gleamed. Near Johnny stood a dark, fearful shape. Its face glowed faintly, and it was a face the professor had seen in old pictures. The lips of the figure moved. It spoke in a horrid, rasping, croaking voice:

"Why have you come here, old fool? This is my time of triumph! You have come to the place where my power is greatest. Soon I will live again, and this detestable creature will die. A fair exchange, they say, is no robbery. What say you? Are you ready for death too?"

The professor was frightened, but he felt anger welling up inside him. "My mother met you once when you were alive!" he roared. "And she said you were the rottenest, meanest creature that ever crawled on the face of the earth! Go back to the dead and leave this poor child alone!"

The professor was amazed at himself. He hadn't expected to say anything like this. But the anger felt good. It cleared his head and made him feel stronger. On the other side of the grassy patch the dark shape hovered, motionless. Then it raised its hand, and the professor felt a numbing shock. And his legs started to move. He was walking forward. He didn't want to go, but he had lost control of the lower part of his body. Frightened, the professor dropped his flashlight. It hit the ground and lay there, still burning. And then—without knowing why he did this—he jammed his right hand into his pants pocket. His fingers closed around his Nimrod pipe lighter. The lighter was a tube about two inches long.

When the two ends were pulled apart, a hole opened in the middle, and flame shot out. Nimrod lighters used a lot of fuel, but they worked in a gale, or in the rain. Fortunately the professor still had control of his hands. He pulled the lighter out and jerked at the ends. A spear of yellow flame shot up into the night. At the same time the professor dug in his heels and struggled as best he could to stop himself.

It worked. He came to a shuddering halt. And the dark shape sprang backward, covering its face with its hands.

The professor looked madly this way and that. He wanted . . . Ah! Glory be to God! Over in a corner of the little lookout place, piled against a cairn of stones, was some wood. But then his heart sank. It had been raining—the wood would be soaked. Frantically, still holding the blazing lighter, he whirled around. And now, for the first time, he saw the cave, a dark hole in the beetling rocky wall. Still holding the lighter up before him, he began to back toward the cave. A few more steps . . . he was in it now. Again he peered around. Ah! Magnificent! Stupendous! Piled in a corner just inside the mouth of the little cave were brush and twigs and sticks. The professor had his firewood after all.

He had to work fast though. The lighter might run out of fuel any minute now, and then where would he be? The professor's mind raced. Tinder. He needed tinder. Some old leathery oak leaves still clung to the broken branches in the pile of firewood. The professor ripped off a handful of them and piled them on the floor of the cave. He touched the lighter to the leaves, and they blazed. Working with mad, headlong speed, the professor snapped his lighter shut and raced over into the corner of the cave. He came back with handfuls of brush and little twigs. The fire grew. The twigs crackled merrily, and now he was throwing on thicker pieces of wood. Every now and then he glanced nervously outside. His flashlight lay where it had fallen. It still cast a line of pale light out across the grass. But except for that he could see nothing.

Now the fire was burning well. The professor stuck a broken branch into it, and it blazed. Armed with the branch, he stepped out into the open. Johnny had been standing in the middle of the little grassy space. But he was not there anymore. Sick with fear, the professor rushed forward. There stood Johnny, at the very edge of the precipice. One more step and he would plunge thousands of feet to his death. With a quick dash the professor made it to where he was standing. He grabbed Johnny's arm just as he was going over the edge and hauled him back to safety.

The professor turned. One hand was clenched tight around Johnny's arm. The other hand grasped the burning branch. It was raining lightly now, and the drops hissed in the fire, but the fire did not go out. Nearby, just outside the circle of light, hovered the dark figure. Its eyes were pinpoints of red light. Johnny sagged to the ground. His body was a dead weight. Stooping, the professor grasped Johnny under the right armpit. Slowly, painfully, he dragged him back toward the cave. He still held the blazing branch up with his free hand. It seemed to take forever, but finally they made it. And just in time too, because the rain was really pelting down now, and it was putting out the fire on the branch. With a sudden thrust the professor heaved the smoldering branch at the red-eyed figure that still hovered menacingly in the darkness. "Take that, you rotten thing!" the professor growled. Immediately he was sorry he had thrown the branch. He was going to need all the wood he could find.

Inside the cave the professor squatted. A pile of sticks lay near him, and he fed them, one by one, into the crackling fire. Beyond the shimmering wall of flame lay darkness. Darkness, and something else. The professor glanced anxiously to his right. There lay Johnny, cold and still. An awful thought occurred to the professor. Was he . . . *No, no, it couldn't be, he wouldn't allow it!* And suddenly a new thought came to the professor. He felt like a fool for not thinking of it before. He shuffled over toward Johnny on his knees and raised his limp left hand. Slowly he began working the ring off of the finger. It didn't want to come off, but the professor had strong hands. Bit by bit it moved, and then it was off. Johnny groaned. He opened his eyes and blinked and looked around blearily.

"Wha . . . where . . ." he muttered thickly.

The professor was overjoyed. Tears sprang to his eyes. "Thank God, thank God . . ." he whispered. He looked at the ring that lay in his hand. The stone was as dull and dark as a chip of coal. It did not even reflect the firelight. The professor had a great urge to fling the ring into the fire, but he thought better of it, so he stuffed it into his pants pocket. Someday some expert on magic might tell him what to do with the ring—if he lived to tell his experiences to anyone.

Right now there was a problem. The fire was keeping the evil creature at bay, but what would happen when the fire went out? Maybe the creature would have to vanish at dawn, but how far away was that? The professor hadn't brought his watch with him, and he hadn't noticed the time when he dashed out of the cottage. He looked at the pitifully small pile of wood, and he felt panic rising inside him.

Meanwhile Johnny was slowly returning to the world. He was bewildered and scared. Only a moment ago, or so it seemed to him, he had fallen asleep in his nice comfortable bed in the motel. Now he was in this dank, dark place where firelight leaped on the walls. And the professor was here too. What on earth had happened?

The professor would have comforted Johnny, but he had no time to be soothing and friendly. His mind was racing as he tried—tried desperately—to think his way out of the mess they were in. The professor believed in thought. He was always telling his students that you could get to the unknown by using the known. If you just put the facts that you knew together in the proper way, you might get some truly amazing results. *All right,* he said to himself grimly as he fed another stick into the fire, *what do you know?* Well, he knew that the ghost was there, outside the cave, waiting. And the ghost had said that he was strongest in this place. *Why?* Why was he strongest here, on the side of Hellbent Mountain, Why? Why? Why?

The professor scrambled to his feet. He began to pace back and forth while Johnny watched him, bleary-eyed and astounded. The professor's thoughts had run up against a blank wall. As he well knew, there are times when logic will not do you the least little tiny bit of good. So he let his mind ramble. It began to leap from one absurd thought to the next. He found that he was humming "Angels From the Realms of Glory," an old Christmas carol. How did it go?

> Angels, from the realms of glo-ry,
> Wing your flight o'er all the earth;
> Ye who sang cre-a-tion's sto-ry,
> Rum te-e dum and diddle durf . . .

It went something like that, anyway. From there, the Professor's mind leapt to the sign he had seen on the trail:

TO THE ANGEL SCENIC VIEW

What was this angel, anyway? High above their heads was the formation known as the Hag. But hags are not angels—that was a well-known fact. So the sign probably referred to some other rock formation. Hmm. Hmmm.

Now the professor found himself thinking about the note that had been found on Father Baart's desk the day he had disappeared, the note that had been a quotation from Sir Thomas Browne's *Urne-Buriall:*

> *The man of God lives longer without a Tomb than any by one, invisibly interred by Angels; and adjudged to obscurity, though not without some marks directing human discovery.*

Again the professor returned to the fire. He crouched down and fed more wood in. There were only a few twigs left, and the fire would use them up in no time. He looked out through the shimmering waves of heat and the orange flames, but he could see nothing. Nothing but darkness and falling rain. *Angels . . . angels . . . interred by angels. . . .* What on God's green earth did that have to do with Father Baart? The quotation referred to Moses, whose body had been carried away by angels. That was what the Bible said, anyway. Moses had been buried in some secret place. Well, now: What about Father Baart? His body had never been found. *Interred by angels . . . interred by angels . . .* What if . . .

Suddenly the professor was down on his knees, scrabbling madly at the hard dirt floor of the cave. He had no tools, only his fingers, and this made digging difficult. Johnny, watching groggily, decided that the professor must have gone completely out of his mind.

"Hey, Professor!" he called. "Whatcha doin'?"

"I'm digging!" the professor yelled over his shoulder. "And you should dig too! Dig over there? Use your hands! Use anything! But hurry! We haven't got much time!"

Johnny didn't understand why he was supposed to dig, but he did as he was told. He grabbed a broken piece of wood and began gouging at the floor of the cave. Dirt flew, and dust rose in a choking cloud. It was a strange scene, the two of them scraping away like dogs looking for bones. Gouge, gouge, scrape, scrape! Johnny wielded the stick like a trowel, and before long he had dug a pretty good-sized trough in the hard-packed dirt floor. But he had to stop because his glasses were covered with steam and powdery dirt. He laid down the stick and pulled out his handkerchief. Then he took off his glasses and wiped them and put them back on. Johnny looked down. He did a double take and looked again. At the bottom of the trough he had made, he could see stone. Rough, flat stone, part of a slab maybe. And imbedded in the stone was something that glimmered faintly in the firelight. A coin. A gold coin, it looked like.

"Hey, Professor!" Johnny yelled. "Come over here! Come over here quick!"

The professor looked up. His fingers were bleeding and sore, and his eyes were wild. "What? What? What is it?"

"I dunno, only . . . only I think you better come over here quick!"

The professor stumbled to his feet. He hurried over to

where Johnny was kneeling and dropped to his knees beside him. The professor's mouth fell open. "It's a coin," he said wonderingly. Then he looked closer. He brushed dirt away with his fingers and winced as he did this, because his fingertips were rubbed raw from the digging. Now he pulled out his Nimrod lighter again and snapped it open. He held the flame down close to the coin, and then he let out a loud, joyous whoop. The professor knew a lot about old coins, and he knew that this was an Elizabethan gold coin called an angel. On the side that was up, there was a picture of an angel. He had wings and a halo and a spear in his hand, and he was killing a dragon with the spear.

"An angel, by God!" roared the professor. He turned to Johnny and grabbed the stick from his hand. Madly he jabbed at the earth with the stick. "We've got to get this stone up!" he muttered feverishly. "We've got to, we've *got to*!!"

Meanwhile behind them the fire burned low. It had collapsed into a heap of red coals. And beyond the fire, at the mouth of the cave, a fearful shape hovered. Johnny turned and looked, and he went rigid with terror. He opened and closed his mouth and tried to speak to the professor, but nothing came out. The professor went on flailing with the stick. At last he had uncovered the ragged edges of the flat stone. He forced his sore, bleeding fingers down into the dirt and pried with them. "Oh, God, oh, God!" he breathed, and he gasped and winced because of the pain in his fingers. But he got a grip on the stone and forced it up. Underneath was a dark hollow space. The professor plunged his hands down into the hole. He came up with a small wooden box. He handed it to Johnny, and then, suddenly, he seemed to become aware of something.

There was very little light in the cave now. The fire was down to a few smoky red embers, and there was no wood left.

"Johnny! Pick up the lighter! Quick!" The professor's voice was feverish.

Johnny set the box down on the ground. He looked around frantically. "I can't see it! Where is it?"

"There! There! God's teeth, man, can't you see it? It's right down by my knee! Hurry! *Hurry!*"

Johnny scrabbled around in the dirt, and his hand closed over a small cold metal object. He had seen the professor use the lighter many times, so he knew how it worked. He tugged at the ends of the cylinder, and there was a snap and a tiny white spark, but nothing else happened. He tried again and again and again. But the lighter was out of fuel. And behind them the last red coal of the fire winked out. Now Johnny felt his flesh go goose-pimply all over. And he smelled a horrid, sickening odor, the odor of corruption. Johnny and the professor turned. At the mouth of the cave they saw a face. An ugly, cruel, grinning face. It was lit by an unearthly light, and it hovered in the thick darkness.

The professor sprang to his feet. "Go away!" he yelled. "Go away, you rotten thing, you filthy, evil—"

But the professor never finished his sentence. A shadowy hand stretched out toward him, and as Johnny watched in horror the professor *disintegrated*. His body turned to dust, and his empty clothes fell in a heap and lay there on the cavern floor.

CHAPTER TWELVE

Johnny was stunned. He was numb with horror. What had happened was so awful that he could hardly believe it. The professor was gone. There was not even a body left. Just a heap of clothes. And now the nightmarish face of Father Baart floated closer.

"It is your turn now," said the croaking voice. "You must die so that I may return to the sweet land of the living. Stand and face me! *I command you to obey!*"

Johnny hesitated. He was frightened half out of his mind, but he was angry too. Ferociously angry. Tears sprang to his eyes. He wanted to throw something—a rock or a boulder— at the horrid mask that floated before his eyes. With a sudden lunge he reached out and grabbed the small wooden box. He leaped to his feet and threw it. The wood of the box was rotten, and it disintegrated as the box flew through the air. And suddenly the air was full of dust. The grinning mask crumpled like a paper lantern thrust into a fire. And then there was a blinding flash of red light and a deep *boom* that seemed to come from far, far down in the bowels of the mountain. The floor of the cave began to shake and tremble and jump crazily about. Clots of dirt and pebbles fell from the ceiling of the cave. Johnny looked around, panic-stricken. What could he do? Suddenly the floor of the cave heaved, and Johnny was sent sprawling. He fell across something soft, something that cried out with a loud crabby voice.

"For the love of God, would you stop kicking me? What do you think I am, anyway?"

Johnny could not believe his ears. The voice was the professor's voice! He was there, alive, lying under Johnny!

With a loud triumphant yell Johnny scrambled to his feet. He was so excited and overjoyed that he hardly knew what he was doing. "Professor? Is that really you?"

The familiar raspy voice responded. "Of course it's me! Who else would it be up here in this disgusting, dank, smelly cave? I came all the way up here to rescue you, and the least you could do is—"

The professor's speech was cut off by a sickening jolt. Once again the cave floor heaved, and more rocks and pebbles came raining down. Now the professor was on his feet. "*Outside!*" he yelled, and grabbing Johnny's arm, he hauled him out through the mouth of the cave. The mountain went on shaking and shivering. It was very dark outside, and it was still raining, but from somewhere far above them Johnny and the professor heard a drumming, thundering roar that grew louder and louder by the second. In terror they clutched each other and waited. It was a rockslide, another rockslide. Down the side of the mountain, boulders came crashing, thundering, and rolling. The din was terrific. Johnny and the professor put their hands over their ears and closed their eyes. Any second now they would be killed, crushed by tons of rock—or so they thought. But then the din died away. From far below they heard splashes and more rumbling. Then came silence.

Johnny opened his eyes and took his hands away from his ears. He was soaked with rain, and it was still black as pitch outside, but he knew that the avalanche had passed them by. He turned to the professor excitedly. "Hey, Professor!" he yelled. "Hey, we're safe! We're safe! The ghost is gone! Hey, you were great, you really were! I thought you were dead, but you're alive! It's wonderful! Whee! Whee!" He waved his arms and started dancing around on the grass.

The professor stood stock still. He smiled faintly. "Oh, I assure you, it was nothing!" he said with a modest wave of his hand.

And then he fainted dead away.

When the professor woke up, he found Johnny kneeling over him. He looked very anxious. It was getting light out. The sky was blue again, and the sun was rising from a reddish haze over on the other side of a wide valley. Birds were twittering in a crooked little juniper tree that grew near the mouth of the cave.

"Are you all right, Professor?" Johnny asked.

The professor sat up. He harrumphed and looked at Johnny, and then he quickly looked away. Plainly he was embarrassed. Fainting was not the sort of thing he usually did. "I'm perfectly all right," he snapped, brushing dirt off his sleeves. "And by the way, what is all that nincompoopery about me being dead? Do I look dead to you? Eh? Do I?"

Johnny explained to the professor as well as he could what he had seen—or rather, what he *thought* he had seen—inside the cave.

"Well, well, well!" said the professor. He cocked his head to one side and looked thoughtful. "It must have been an illusion. Old Shagnasty must've known that we had him in a corner. We were within an inch of victory when we found the box that had his ashes in it. He wanted you to despair and give up. I'm so glad you didn't!"

"So'm I," said Johnny. Once again there were tears in his eyes, and he shuddered as he realized how narrow their escape had been.

The professor got to his feet. Fussily he brushed off the seat of his pants and his trouser legs. He glanced this way and that. "By the way," he said, "what was all that godawful noise? When I woke up from . . . from whatever happened to me, it seemed like the whole bloody mountain was coming down around our ears."

Johnny pointed off to the right. It was not hard to see the path that the rockslide had made. A great raw gash ran down the rugged face of the mountain. The falling stones and boulders had wiped out what was left of the trail. Johnny and the professor would have to be rescued by somebody, somehow.

"Heavenly days, McGee!" exclaimed the professor in wonder. He walked to the edge of the drop-off and looked down. The path of the rockslide continued down the steep side of the mountain. Far down, near the bottom, you could see where trees had been mowed down by the rolling boulders. The professor squinted and strained to see, but his eyes were not good for distances. "Tell me, John," he said, beckoning for Johnny to come closer, "are those boulders in the lake way down there?"

Johnny walked to the edge and looked. "Yeah . . . yeah, I guess so," he said uncertainly. He turned and pointed up. "They came from up there."

The professor looked where Johnny was pointing, and then, in a flash, it hit him. He knew what had happened. The Hag had come down. The jutting, shelving boulders that formed the face of the Hag had been dislodged by the earthquake, and now they were down in Hag Lake, thousands of feet below. The professor started to laugh. He couldn't help it—it all seemed terribly funny. He thought about all the things that had been named for the Hag. He thought about Hag View Cottages and Hag Kumfy Kabins and pieces of pine-scented soap shaped like the Hag and most of all of Hagtooth Harry's trained bears. It was just a stitch, it really was.

When the professor's laughing fit had died down, Johnny asked timidly, "Did . . . did the ghost make the earthquake happen?"

The professor was startled by this question. Now all the things that had happened last night came flooding back into his mind, and he grew serious again. "Yes," he said, nodding, "or rather, his passing caused the earth to shake. But he's gone now, gone for good. At least, I hope—" The professor paused. He had been gazing vaguely around while he talked. Now he found that he was looking at a funny-shaped outcropping of rock that rose above the entrance to the cave. The morning sun was shining on the eastern flank of the mountain, and it touched the ragged finger of rock with golden fire. The rock looked like an angel. It had wings and a head and even something that looked a bit like an outstretched hand.

"*Interred by angels* . . ." muttered the professor, nodding. "One was up there, and the other was a coin. Clever, clev-*er*! But I wonder who planted him up here? Who did the burying, I mean?"

Johnny had not understood anything that the professor

said. Not that it mattered much to him at the moment. He was just happy to be alive. He still did not understand how he managed to travel from his bed at the motel to this wild, lonely place in the mountains. But he knew it all had something to do with the ghost of Father Baart—who had turned out to be real, after all. And he also knew—or hoped—that the professor would explain everything to him in good time.

Right now, however, there were other problems. "How're we gonna get down, Professor?" Johnny asked.

The professor made a puckery face. "Oh, I suspect that we will have company shortly," he said dryly. "Earthquakes are not common up here in the White Mountains, and when the local yokels see what has happened to their chief tourist attraction, there'll be lots of people swarming all over the mountain, taking pictures and saying tsk-tsk and standing around with their mouths hanging open. So don't worry. In the meantime, however, we will have to wait. It'll be boring, I know, but it beats plunging thousands of feet to our death. Don't you agree?"

Johnny agreed. So he sat down on the dewy grass with the professor, and they talked about this and that as the sun rose higher and higher. In the middle of their conversation the professor got up and went into the cave. He came back with the slab of stone that had the gold coin embedded in it. He remarked sadly to Johnny that Elizabethan gold angels were much prized by coin collectors. Then he added that the coin had lain for years over the grave of a wicked sorcerer. And after that the professor took the slab to the edge of the precipice and heaved it over, coin and all. Then he went back and sat down next to Johnny on the grass and talked some more. Presently they began to hear a *whap-whap* sound in the air and the whirring of motors. They looked up and saw a helicopter. It was coming down over the top of Hellbent Mountain.

Johnny and the Professor sprang to their feet and began yelling and waving frantically. The helicopter hovered briefly near the top of the mountain, and then, slowly, it moved closer. It floated down onto the grassy patch while its whirling propeller stirred up a mighty wind. The engine sounds died, and the propeller spun to a halt. A door in the cabin of the copter opened, and a state trooper climbed out. He was a man about sixty years old, with a leathery, seamed, sunburnt face and a gray crew cut. He wore the green uniform of the New Hampshire State Police, and when he opened his mouth, he talked with a heavy New Hampshire accent.

"Hi, there!" he said, waving. "I bet you guys was wonderin' how you was gonna get down, wasn't you?" He turned and peered down over the edge of the chasm. Then he let out a long, low whistle and shook his head gravely. "Gonna be hard on the tourist business," he said mournfully. "What in heck you think people'll come up here to see now?"

The professor thought of the towering, rugged mountains, and how they looked in autumn, when their sides were alight with colors, yellow and orange and red. He thought of the mountain streams and steep gorges and the layers of brown needles covering the forest floor. He thought of the mountains in moonlight, and lonely night drives along the Kankamagus Highway.

"Oh, I imagine there'll be *something* to look at," he said sarcastically. "There's always Hagtooth Harry's trained bears, after all."

The policeman sighed and shook his head. "Kids'll be awful disappointed," he said. Then he added, as an after-thought, "You folks like a ride back, would you?"

The professor and Johnny climbed into the helicopter with the trooper and rode back with him to the motel. Johnny enjoyed the ride tremendously. He had only been in an airplane once before in his life, and he had never ridden in a helicopter. The professor closed his eyes and spent his time trying to remember the kings and queens of England and which one came after which. After an amazingly short ride the copter set them down on the front lawn of the Hag View Cottages. But as soon as they stepped out onto solid ground again, Johnny and the professor ran into more trouble. A State Police cruiser was pulled up in front of the cottage they were staying in. The owner, a bald, red-faced man with a big overhanging beer belly, was talking excitedly with two policemen. When he saw the two missing persons walk-ing toward him, he nearly had a conniption fit.

"*Jeezus!*" he exclaimed in a loud foghorn voice. "Where'd *you* two come from? Gawd, I thought you two was at the bottom o' Hag Lake or someplace! What happened to ya? Huh?"

On the spur of the moment the professor made up a cock-and-bull story: He explained to the owner that Johnny was nervous and excitable. He had been under a doctor's care recently because of the loss of his mother. Last night, for no reason at all, Johnny had plunged out into the night, and the professor had followed after, and then the two of them had got trapped by the earthquake and had to be rescued.

The owner accepted the story—at least he said that he did—but he glowered suspiciously at the professor. The professor didn't know it, but he had been under suspicion from the time he signed the register in the motel's office. He had signed it "Roderick Childermass, Ph.D.," and as far as the owner was concerned, all Ph.D.'s were kooks and Communists and God knows what else. As for the policemen, they were just glad that they could call off the search and go home.

After the policemen had gone and everyone had calmed down a bit, Johnny and the professor packed their bags and got ready to leave. The professor went to the motel office and paid the bill, and off they went. They drove straight back to Duston Heights, stopping only in the town of Rochester to grab lunch at a drive-in. When the professor's car pulled up in front of the Dixon house, Gramma and Grampa knew right away that something had happened. The travelers had come back from their trip two days early, and they had come back suddenly, without calling, without explanations. At first Johnny and the professor were very secretive and close-mouthed about what had happened. Finally, though, the professor admitted that something very strange and mysterious and scary had happened. And he said that he'd tell the Dixons the whole story in three days time. In the meantime he needed to make a few phone calls and confer with a friend of his. Then—after grabbing a Bible out of a bookcase and making Johnny swear to secrecy on it—the professor left.

Three days passed. During this time Johnny stayed at home. He did jigsaw puzzles and played cribbage and checkers with Grampa. Meanwhile across the street the professor was busy. First he called up Dr. Melkonian and chewed him out. Without giving the doctor a chance to get a word in edgewise, he told him that he was a pompous, posturing bearded hornswoggler, who ought to have his psychiatric license revoked. He accused him of mystagogic muckification and pointless prattle, and he said that he'd ask for his money back if he thought that there was any chance it'd be returned. He ended up by slamming the receiver down hard in the doctor's ear. This little rant did not make a whole lot of sense, but it left the professor feeling relieved and curiously satisfied. Next the professor hired a cleaning lady to whip his house into shape so he could have visitors in. Finally he made a long-distance call to an old friend of his up in Durham, New Hampshire, the town where the University of New Hampshire is.

On a Friday night at around eight o'clock Gramma, Grampa, and Johnny went across the street to the professor's house. When he met them at the door, he was wearing a red damask smoking jacket that smelled of mothballs, and he was smoking Balkan Sobranie tobacco in a pipe—he had decided that cigarettes were bad for his health. The professor ushered his guests into the living room. A bright fire burned in the fireplace, and the crystal pendants on the ormolu candlesticks on the mantel glistened and glittered. In an easy chair by the fire someone was sitting—a stranger. He was a tall, weedy man with a fluff of white hair on his head. He wore big, goggly, horn-rimmed glasses, and his long pointed nose was bent and ridged. The shoulders of his tweed jacket were covered with dandruff, and the elbows had leather patches. His pants were baggy and shapeless, and his long pointed shoes looked as if they were made out of cardboard.

"This is Professor Charles Coote," said Professor Childermass, pointing toward the man. "He is an old friend of mine, and he has written a very important book on Egyptian magic. He also knows a great deal about *ushabti*—of which we shall have more to say later."

Professor Coote stood up and made three quick nods of his head: one toward Johnny, one toward Gramma, and one toward Grampa. Then he sat down and folded his hands in his lap. Professor Childermass led Gramma and Grampa over to the sofa and asked them to sit down.

Johnny sat down on a straight chair and squirmed impatiently. He did not know what the professor was going to say or do, and he was impatient and extremely curious.

The professor took his pipe out of his mouth and harrumphed. He looked around as if he didn't know where he was, and then, with a sudden abrupt dash, he went to the sideboard and came back with a rattling tray full of bottles and glasses. He set the tray down on the coffee table with a jolt, and then he backed away into the middle of the room. Entertaining people was a chore for the professor. He didn't do it often, and whenever he did it, he acted as if he was trying to get things over with as quickly as possible.

"Well, uh . . . just help yourselves," he said, waving his hand awkwardly. "There's . . . well, there's sherry for those who drink it, and imitation nonalcoholic sherry-flavored punch for those who, uh, like that sort of, uh, thing. Just . . . uh, help yourselves." When this little speech was over, the professor retreated to the fireplace and stood there, fidgeting. Professor Coote got up and loped across the room to the coffee table. He poured himself a glass of sherry and went back to his chair. Then everyone else started to help themselves. Johnny wanted a glass of sherry, but he could tell from the look in Gramma's eye that he'd better have some of the other stuff instead.

When everybody had something to drink, the professor poured himself a glass of sherry. He downed it all in one gulp, wiped his mouth with the back of his hand, and slammed the glass down on the mantelpiece. After some harrumphing and nose blowing he turned again to face his company and began to speak. He had called them here, he said, to clear up some of the mysteries of the last few months. First he wanted Johnny to speak.

"Who, me, Professor?" Johnny asked, tapping his chest with his finger.

The professor nodded. "Yes, you, my friend. I want you to begin at the beginning and tell these folks everything you can remember about the whole crazy business that you have been mixed up in."

Johnny thought about the figurine that he had stolen from the church. He glanced nervously at Gramma and Grampa. "Do I have to tell . . . *everything*?" he asked.

"Yes," said the professor firmly. "Everything! Don't leave out a jot or a tittle or a smidgin. And don't worry. No one's going to disown you or clap you in irons. Please begin."

So Johnny told his tale. He told about how he had stolen the figurine from the church. He told about Mr. Beard and the ring and the weird and ghostly things that had happened to him after he put the ring on his finger and began saying the prayer to Thoth and Touëris. Finally he told about what had happened to him and the professor up on Hellbent Mountain at midnight, amid lightning and thunder and rain. Of course, since Johnny had been unconscious or sleepwalking during part of this last episode, the professor had to fill in details. He did this in a very dramatic way, with lots of gestures. Finally, when Johnny and the professor had both said their piece, silence fell. There was no sound in the room but the crackling of the fire. Then Gramma stirred restlessly in her seat. She gave Grampa a hard nudge in the ribs with her elbow and said to him in an accusing tone, "How about *that*, eh, Mr. Smarty-pants? Mr. Know-it-all? You're the one that said the ghost was just a lot o' foofaraw, an' I was just an old superstitious Irish lady. What d'ye say now? Eh?"

Grampa groaned. "I think I'm gonna be hearin' about this for the next six months," he said, and he gave Johnny a humorous look, as if to say "What're you gonna do?"

Gramma turned to the professor next. She gave him her best glower, as if she felt everything that had happened was his fault. "Them spiders," she began, wrinkling up her nose in disgust, "was . . . was they somethin' that came with the blue doojigger in the black box?"

The professor turned to Professor Coote and grinned. "You're on, Charley," he said. "Help the lady."

Professor Coote spoke up. He sounded very scholarly and precise. "In a manner of speaking, yes. They were a manifestation of the forces—the evil forces— that dwelt inside the blue figurine. Insects have often been associated with evil spirits. Beelzebub was one of the Seven Devils, and his name means 'Lord of the Flies.' "

"What was that blue thing, anyway?" Grampa asked. "Did old Baart make it, or was it a souvenir?"

Once again Professor Coote responded. "No, in spite of that label he put on to confuse people, it was a genuine *ushabti*. A tomb figurine. But it was not Egyptian. It came from Kush, which is an ancient kingdom far up the Nile, beyond Egypt. The kings of Kush conquered Egypt in the eighth century B.C., and they ruled there for a while. When they were driven out, they carried Egyptian customs back to Kush with them. Then, when they were back in their own little kingdom, the Kushites pretended that they were Egyptians. They followed Egyptian religious practices, wrote Egyptian hieroglyphics, and they made *ushabti*. Of course, the workmanship of these *ushabti* was rather crude." He turned to the professor and smiled patronizingly. "No doubt, Roderick," he added, "that is why you failed to see that the *ushabti* was genuine. A genuine ancient object, I mean."

The professor scowled. "Oh, don't be silly, Charley," he snapped. "I wouldn't have known a genuine Egyptian *ushabti* if it bit me on the rear. But like most scholars, I like to pretend that I know more than I really know. So I screwed up. Shut your trap and have more sherry."

There was an awkward silence. Professor Coote blew his nose, and then he made a dash for the coffee table. He refilled his glass and hurried back to his seat.

Grampa still had some questions to ask. "Look, Rod," he said, pointing a long freckled finger at the professor, "if that blue doohickey was really ancient, where'd old Baart get his hands on it? D'ye think that guy, that wood-carver, gave it to him?"

The professor stuck his hands in his pockets and shrugged. "I think that the wood-carver must have given the figurine to Father Baart. By the way, would you care to see it—or rather, what's left of it?"

Gramma, Grampa, and Johnny all said "Yeah!" or "Sure!" or "You're darn tootin'!" together.

The professor walked over to the armchair where Professor Coote was sitting. Down on the floor, hidden by the shadow of the armchair, lay a large black book. Stooping, the professor picked the book up and carried it out into the center of the room. Johnny, Gramma, and Grampa all leaned forward eagerly to look as the professor flipped the heavy cover back. Inside the book lay the shattered, charred fragments of the blue figurine.

"My gosh!" Johnny exclaimed. "Did you do that to it, Professor?"

The professor shook his head. "Nope. I found the figurine like this when I got back home from our trip. I think it must have happened when you scattered the ashes of our dear old friend Father Baart. The ring got the same treatment. I took it out of my pocket when I paid our bill at the motel, and it looked like this."

He reached into the pocket of his smoking jacket and took out a twisted wad of blackened metal. "The stone was gone," he added as he showed the remains of the ring around. "It vaporized, or exploded, or something. I found little bits of fingernail parings and hair—I think that's what they were. They were clinging to the metal part of the ring, and I imagine they were under the stone. I burned them in my fireplace, which is the proper thing to do with such rubbish, I believe."

"Yes," said Professor Coote, nodding. "I believe you did the right thing." He smiled prissily and added, "You also ought to bury the remains of the *ushabti* and the ring. Bury the pieces under the roots of a yew tree in a cemetery by the light of a new moon. That is the method of disposing of cursed objects that is recommended by the great astrologer Regiomontanus. He says that—"

"You mean Johannes Müller of Königsberg, don't you?" said the professor, interrupting. "That's his real name, you know."

Professor Coote gave his friend a dirty look. "Yes, I *know* what his real name is. But it would be stuffy and pedantic to call him Johannes Müller, wouldn't it? And we wouldn't want to be stuffy and pedantic, would we?" Professor Coote had been looking for some way of getting even for the "shut your trap" remark. Now he sat back in his chair, satisfied.

Johnny spoke up again at this point. There was still a lot about this business that seemed puzzling to him. "How come old Father Baart wanted to kill me?" he asked. "Was it just because he was evil, or what?"

The professor studied the burning tobacco in the bowl of his pipe. "I think," he said slowly, "that it was going to be a case of a life for a life. Baart was dead, you see.

He was an evil sorcerer, and he made some mistake in the middle of his sorcerizing. What he did wrong we'll never ever know, but it got him killed. His body was burnt to ashes, and it was buried up in the mountains by . . . by whom? The wood-carver? The Powers of Darkness? I don't suppose we'll ever know. But to continue: Baart was dead, but his spirit still hung around on the earth. He haunted St. Michael's Church, and he would have gone on haunting it—harmlessly—forever, I suppose. But you took the lid off the cauldron, Johnny. You disregarded the warning and took the figurine out of the church. A church is a sacred place. It can keep the powers of evil in check. But once you removed the figurine from the protection of the church, then—quite literally—all hell broke loose. And what did our old pal Baart want? He wanted to be *alive* again in the world. So he appeared to you as Mr. Beard, and he gave you a ring. And the ring gave you power, power against bullies like Eddie, but that was not its real purpose. No. The ring gave Baart power over *you*. It was part of his plan. With the ring on your finger you were going to die at midnight in Duston Park, and he was going to come back to the world of the living. In what form, I wonder? As young Johnny Dixon? As Father Baart? As Mr. Beard? God only knows."

Johnny shuddered. "He said I would die if I took the ring off my finger. That's why I kept it on."

The professor grimaced. "That was just a lot of threatening folderol, my boy. You could have taken the ring off whenever you wanted to. Actually the situation was just the opposite of what that old devil said it was. You would die if you *did* keep the ring on your finger. So it was really very fortunate that . . . that . . ."

The professor's voice trailed away. He suddenly became very gloomy and bit his lip.

"What's the matter, Professor?" Johnny asked anxiously.

The professor heaved a deep despairing sigh. He walked to the fireplace and knocked his pipe out against one of the andirons. "Oh, nothing," he said sadly. "Nothing much. It just suddenly occurred to me that Dr. Melkonian probably saved your life. He took the ring off, as you know, when you were asleep in his office. If you had still had the ring on when we went to Duston Park at midnight, the old buzzard would've made short work of you—and of me too, perhaps. And was I nice to Dr. Melkonian? Was I grateful? No. I chewed him out over the phone because he was wrong about what was wrong with you. Sometimes I think I'm really not a very nice person." Tears came to the professor's eyes. It looked as if he was going to break down and bawl right there in front of everybody.

Johnny jumped to his feet. There were tears in his eyes too. "No, Professor!" he exclaimed loudly. "You're not a bad guy! Really, you're not! If you hadn't've come up to rescue me, I'd be dead! You stood right up to the ghost, and you're a real brave guy! Honest, I mean it! Don't cry! Please don't!"

The professor blinked and sniffled. He took out a red cotton handkerchief and blew his nose loudly. "You think I'm okay after all?" he asked, looking around uncertainly.

"Of *course* you're okay!" put in Professor Coote. He reached up from where he was sitting and patted the professor reassuringly on the arm. "You have one of the filthiest tempers I've ever seen in my life, but when you're not screaming and raging or throwing the furniture around, you're an extremely kind and thoughtful person. Of course," he added, poking a forefinger at the professor, "it *would* help your reputation if you'd sit down tomorrow and write a nice note to Dr. Melkonian explaining how you really feel now and apologizing to him for your boorish behavior. I mean, it would be the decent thing to do."

The professor took off his glasses and dabbed at his eyes with his soggy handkerchief. Then he put his glasses back on and looked around the room. Everyone was smiling at him. Grampa was grinning and puffing contentedly at his pipe. Even Gramma, whose normal expression was a frown, was smiling now.

The professor harrumphed and rubbed his elbows. He stuck his pipe back in his mouth and tried to act stuffy. "Hmh!" he snorted. "Well now, is . . . is there anything more I can get for anybody? Eh?"

"There certainly is," said Professor Coote in a dry, sarcastic voice. "I believe it is the custom to serve cookies and other edible goodies with sherry. And indeed, when

I was in your kitchen earlier this evening, I saw a plate loaded with such items. It was sitting on the counter by the sink. And that's where it still is."

The professor's face turned red. He slapped his forehead with the flat of his hand. "Phooey!" he roared. "I *knew* I had forgotten something! Just a minute." He turned on his heel and dashed out of the room. A moment later he returned. In his hands was a china platter, and it was loaded with all sorts of tasty things. Peanut-butter cookies and chocolate brownies with chocolate frosting and chocolate candies (creams—the professor hated caramel fillings) and piles of bonbons on paper doilies. Then the professor went back and came in a second time. This time he was carrying a plate with a Sacher torte on it. A Sacher torte is a kind of super chocolate cake. It has lots of layers, and the spaces between the layers are filled with apricot jam. And on the outside is lots of rich, dark chocolate frosting. The professor had made the Sacher torte the night before, and he had hidden it away in a cupboard to bring out as a surprise. But amid the fuss and flurry of getting ready for guests, he had forgotten all about it.

Now that the serious part of the evening was over with, everybody ate and drank and talked and had a good time. Later Professor Coote wandered upstairs and while looking for the bathroom accidentally discovered the fuss closet. The professor had never told him about the closet, so naturally he wondered what it was for. But when he went downstairs and asked, the professor told him that he was thinking of becoming a Buddhist monk in his old age and was practicing meditation. This explanation did not quite fit the sign on the inside of the closet door, but Professor Coote was not one to pry, so he let it go at that. Then the professor sat down at the piano in the living room and played old songs, and everybody joined in, singing along. Gramma insisted that the professor play "Just a Song at Twilight," and he did, and Gramma got very weepy, because that had been her mother's favorite song. And then the professor played "The Star-Spangled Banner" and told everybody that the evening was over and they had to go home.

Out on the front walk under the stars the professor was saying good-bye to Johnny. Professor Coote was upstairs in bed. He was staying overnight at the professor's house and was going back to Durham in the morning. Gramma and Grampa had already gone back to their house. Johnny didn't want to go—not yet. He kept thinking that there were more things that he wanted to ask the professor. But he was so sleepy and stuffed with goodies that he could not think what these things might be.

"Well, John," said the professor amiably, "you've had quite an adventure! Did you think it was as good as the ones you listen to on the radio? Hmm?"

Johnny made a face. He was thinking that adventures were fine as long as you could sit in your living room and listen to or read about them. "You know what I wish?" he said suddenly.

"What? What do you wish?"

"I wish I had a nice safe kind of magic ring that would keep Eddie Tompke off of my back."

The professor shook his head vigorously. "No, you don't! You don't wish that at all! If you had a ring like that, it would be . . . well, it would be like carrying a loaded pistol around all the time. Sooner or later you'd be tempted to use it in some evil way, and then you'd be horribly sorry afterward. People don't know when they're well off. I knew a fellow in college, and he was fun to be around. But he was all weak and wasty—didn't have any muscles. So he worked out with weights and ran for miles, and he turned into a real rough and tough bruiser. He also turned into one of the biggest bores on the face of the earth. All he would ever talk about was how he had turned himself into a muscleman. Stay like you are. You'll be a lot—"

"John-nee! John-nee!"

Johnny turned and looked. It was Gramma. She was standing on the front steps with her hands cupped to her mouth.

"What is it, Gramma?" he yelled. "What's the matter?"

"It's your father! He's on the phone! He's calling all the way from some place I never heard of! Come on! Hurry!"

Johnny was overjoyed. He hadn't heard from his dad in a long time, and he had been wondering what was happening to him. "Oh, my gosh!" he exclaimed excitedly. "Hey, Professor, I gotta go! Thanks for everything! I . . . g'bye! G'bye!"

He started across the street, but at the curb he came to a sudden halt. He turned and gazed forlornly at the professor. He had just realized that his dad would never, ever believe the stuff he had to tell him.

The professor had read Johnny's thoughts. He started to chuckle. "What's the matter, John?" he asked.

Johnny did not see what was so funny. "What'm I gonna tell him, Professor? My dad, I mean. What'll I say?"

The professor thought a second. "Tell him that you got all A's in school, except for the D you got in penmanship. And don't lie about the D. It's always best to tell the truth."

Johnny stared in astonishment. Then he burst out laughing. Still laughing, he turned and ran back across the street toward the lighted doorway of his house.

ABOUT THE AUTHOR

JOHN BELLAIRS is well known for his gothic thrillers. He is the author of *The House with a Clock in Its Walls; The Figure in the Shadows; The Letter, the Witch, and the Ring;* and *The Mummy, the Will, and the Crypt,* which is a sequel to this book. The first two titles were both chosen by *The New York Times* as Outstanding Books of the Year.

Mr. Bellairs has also written several adult books, among them *The Face in the Frost* and *The Pedant and the Shuffly.*

He grew up in Michigan and lives in Haverhill, Massachusetts. Mr. Bellairs is currently working on another scary book.

WANT TO READ THE
MOST EXCITING BOOKS AROUND?
CHOOSE CHOOSE YOUR OWN ADVENTURE®

Everybody loves Bantam Skylark CHOOSE
YOUR OWN ADVENTURE® books because the
stories are about *you*. Each book is loaded with
choices that only *you* can make. Instead of